New Sun Rising: Ten Stories

By Lindsay Edmunds

New Sun Rising: Ten Stories
Copyright © 2015 by Lindsay Edmunds
All rights reserved.
No part of this publication may be reproduced without written permission from the publisher. For information visit:
www.lindsayedmunds.com

These stories are works of fiction. Names, characters, places, and incidents are either the product of the author's imagination or are used fictitiously. Any resemblance to actual events, locales, or persons, living or dead, is coincidental.

Editors: Jude Tingley, Crystal Watanabe, Jill Groce
Cover by Dave Hunter
Cover photo by James Birkbeck

Dedicated to the memory of Shirley Jackson, Russell Hoban, Evan S. Connell, and Ray Bradbury, in whose mighty shadows these stories walk.

Summary

These ten stories center around sixteen-year-old Kedzie Greer, who leaves her utopian hometown to make her way in a dystopian society. The time is 2199; the place is the Reunited States.

Kedzie finds a job that horrifies her parents, who think they raised her too well and protected her too much. They fear she is not suited for life anywhere BUT their idyllic town.

When Kedzie talks about choosing a better life, she finds herself with an audience eager to listen. Followers flock to her as if she were Joan of Arc.

However, *New Sun Rising* is not another "teenager with special powers saves the world" book.

The stories are told from multiple points of view. Kedzie's frightened parents, her cynical coworkers, her corrupt boss, and the e-beasts who control the Reunited States through puppet governors all have something to say about this charismatic and courageous girl.

These stories are meant to be read in order. Story 1, first; story 2, second, etc.

Contents

1 - The Town With Four Names	1
2 - Leaving Home	17
3 - Julia and Adele	38
4 - Human Warehouse #44	48
5 - Banner Boles's Obsession	80
6 - Fallow Time	91
7 - All for Love	114
8 - Is Four Enough? Is Six Too Many?	125
9 - The E-beasts Get Mad	135
10 - New Sun Rising	154
Other Works	173
About the Author	175

Acknowledgments

New Sun Rising benefited from the work of three editors. Jude Tingley saw the stories first, when they were, to put it kindly, "unfinished." Her comments invariably pointed me in the right direction. Crystal Watanabe suggested the right changes in the right places and gave me more than one great concluding line. Jill Groce put the polish on the final product.

New Sun Rising represents my fifth collaboration with graphic artist Dave Hunter. Once again, he designed a fine cover.

Thanks to Susan Dormady Eisenberg, who read early versions of these stories and believed in their worth.

Thanks also to an author I've never met: Susan Kaye Quinn. She writes speculative fiction that has many enthusiastic readers, including me. As I follow her career, I keep having Aha! moments such as "I never thought of this" and "That's a good idea; I'll try it."

A funny thing about success: I want it as much for the people who helped me as for myself.

1

The Town With Four Names

Summer, sweet as clover, honey-grass, and wild mint, kept its lovely time.
—Ray Bradbury, *Something Wicked This Way Comes*

Cassie Stillwater looked at a photo of her ancestor, Garvis Stillwater. It showed a pleasant-looking, middle-aged man in a frock coat and tie. His eyes were fixed on the middle distance, as if he were beholding something unseen by the camera. "As perhaps you were," Cassie said to the photo. "No. As you surely were." She sighed and picked up the pages she had written. At age ninety, she was too old to write a memoir, possibly too old to write anything. No matter. The work seemed important. For more than three hundred years, Stillwaters had been the town's witnesses. They knew it when it was New Albion, Cloodyville, and Green Man, and finally when it became Stillwater in 2118. They had seen it nearly destroyed after the Second Civil War. They had seen it rise like a phoenix.

She had labored so hard to find the right words. Once, at five in the morning, hard at work, she realized that her heart had stopped entirely. After a few seconds, it resumed beating. She resumed writing.

In the end, she had not said what she meant. How can any lover explain what is special about their beloved? Her story and the town's story were mixed up together. Perhaps all her labor had resulted in something foolish. An old woman's last thoughts.

Cassie breathed deeply to quiet herself. When her heart stopped knocking on heaven's gate, she went downstairs to make a cup of strong, sugared tea. Sipping it, she felt better. She carried the cup of tea upstairs *to the big front bedroom where some of the deepest experiences of her life had happened. Her wedding night. The births of her three children. The death of her husband.*

At a spindly old desk, placed where she could look out on Star Lake, she had written her story. Now it was finished. She began to read.

~ * ~

Although my town has had four names in the three hundred-odd years of its existence, no one ever troubled to rename the streets. From the beginning, we have had Dulci Alley, Water Street, Stone Street, Geranium Lane, and Revel Road. The four main streets are Wellborne, Angelique, Revere, and Ghost. My house was built by my ancestor Garvis Stillwater, who named it Rose in Bloom. It is on Water Street, along the lakefront. The summer community founded by my ancestor is still part of our identity, but we are a true village now, with year-round residents.

Star Lake is as it has always been: restless, beautiful, and bewitching. I believe it is the source of our town's various spiritualities. The veil between this world and other dimensions is very thin here. *Very thin.* For all we know, our lake is a gateway through which unseen beings pass back and forth. I—who have no coherent religion—become mystical when I see the water. We all do.

From the day it knocked Garvis Stillwater to his knees and got him praying to God for direction, Star Lake has had a way of getting people's attention.

The beginnings of the lake in glacial upheavals are unknowable. Native Americans had a name for it that could not be coherently translated. "When you see me, you will know me" was one stab at it.

On a clear night, the lake mirrors the night sky, as all lakes do. Therefore, early white settlers named it Star Lake.

Star Lake is more than 1300 feet above sea level. Its altitude protects us from the worst heat of the lowlands, but the winters are hard. Sometimes the lake freezes so quickly that individual waves turn into ice sculptures, just like that. A glorious sight to see. In autumn, the lake turns emerald green, with fall colors reflecting in the water. Spring brings refreshment. Summer brings the luxury of long days. When people devoted to progress—meaning personal wealth—tore up everything, they overlooked our small part of the world.

Before he encountered Star Lake, Garvis Stillwater was a practical man. A wealthy Midwestern industrialist, he believed in the world he inhabited and no other. Religion in general and Christianity in particular bored him. Then in October 1870, he came east on business and missed his train back to Chicago. Because he had nothing better to do, he took a walk along the lake's western shore. He described the day as full of color. After about a half hour, he found himself on his knees on the rocky shore, praying to the God whom he would have denied a minute ago. He asked for guidance. He got it.

It is all in his book, *New Albion: The Story of an Awakening*.

Garvis Stillwater encountered Star Lake only five years after the end of the First War Between the States. Hope was blooming fiercely and passionately in the bloody dust. Light poured into the cracks opened by loss, death, and suffering. People wanted to put the war behind them. They wanted to better themselves. When Garvis Stillwater founded his summer community devoted to religion and education, he was acting very much in the spirit of his time.

He named it New Albion. Our town's first name lasted for 236 years.

The first residents arrived in carts, trains, and boats to pitch tents in the summer heat. Surrounded by clouds of insects, they lived and prayed together. They talked about ideas and ideals. They shared meals. They made music during the long evenings. They walked the shoreline. They ventured out in rowboats.

New Albion became wildly popular in a way that would be inconceivable today. Cottages replaced the tents. Roads were added, and a village square with small shops. A great outdoor amphitheater rose up, with the capacity to seat five thousand people.

In the town square, Garvis Stillwater built a fountain. In its center an angel seemed to be dancing—her arms uplifted in joy or praise. The photos of that sculpture are extraordinary. The town library has a few of them. I have most of them.

Garvis Stillwater labored for the good of New Albion until the day of his death. I mean that literally. He died at age ninety-one in mid-conversation with a philanthropist about a donation for a new library. The philanthropist, deeply impressed as anyone would have been, wrote a large check and attended the funeral as well. The library is still here.

That day was June 30, 1930. The country was in the midst of its first Great Depression.

The house from which I write these words is where Garvis Stillwater, his wife Beth, and their five children lived year-round. Not many people did that in the first two centuries or so, but he could not bear to be apart from the place that changed his life.

New Albion survived the Depression, though barely. It grew in size and fame. People craved art, music, and recreation. They wanted beautiful places to live and walk. All these things New Albion provided. It acquired a theater, art gallery, cinema, concert hall, chapels, and a great many rooming houses. Our community bloomed during the summer like an enchanted garden, then retreated into rural quietness as the leaves began falling.

New Albion was born in the wake of the First Civil War. It died in the wake of the second.

In the Second Civil War, as in the first, states seceded and human rights were at stake. The particular human right at stake was privacy. A battle also raged over individual versus corporate rights, However, only one side claimed an official belief in God—and it lost. Both sides, godly and godless, used terrorism rather than troops to make their points. Soldiers, even robotic ones, were expensive and unpredictable. Terrorism was cheap. Ordinary citizens going about the business of living could be destroyed with almost no effort at all. Politicians tweet-tweet-tweeted that terror was progress.

What a strange and lonesome thing a "tweet" was.

The war lasted six years, from 2097 to 2103. Billions were spent, millions were killed and ruined. There was economic catastrophe on an unprecedented scale. In the end, times became so bad that neither side could afford to fight anymore.

Someone tossed a small bomb at New Albion, but it landed on the opera house, built in 1923 out of solid concrete. The bomb stubbed its toe and hopped away howling. The opera house continued to be its massive, unperturbed self. If future archaeologists ever discover the ruins of Stillwater, they will see that place still standing and say, "The natives did like their opera."

During and after the Second Civil War, the summer people not murdered by bombs could not afford to come back to New Albion. The town could no longer pay for art and education; it could barely keep the lights on. Spiritual nourishment, too, went deep underground.

Most residents, seasonal and year-round, abandoned their homes or sold them for next to nothing. The few who stayed reverted to pioneer times. They planted vegetable gardens and raised chickens and pigs. They cut ice from the lake in winter for refrigeration. Children died of diseases that used to be preventable. Women died in childbirth. These conditions, you understand, were not unique to New Albion.

The war produced robbers and profiteers, as wars always do, but no one wanted anything to do with our town. Not until the Cloody family came along.

Every one of those Cloodys, including the babies, were billionaires. Far from ruining them, the Second Civil War made them richer than ever. Their original fortune was made by C. R. Cloody, an atheist and libertarian. However, his descendants were fundamentalist Christians. They bought up three-fourths of the town at fire-sale prices with the notion of turning New Albion into a type of Christian re-education camp. Their mission was not only to convert non-Christians, but also to straighten out Christians who practiced their faith incorrectly.

You might ask, "What in God's name (forgive the choice of words) were the Cloodys thinking?" Cloodyville was a fantasy that had no chance of working in any world, never mind the postwar environment in which they launched it.

If I wanted to be fair, I would say that the Cloodys saw the writing on the wall in at least one respect. The Second Civil War did organized religion no favors. The young survivors did not have religion ingrained in them as stringently and shunned God-talk. The older survivors had seen (and sometimes done) hideous things, and many had become cynical. In addition, the victorious side ended the tax-exempt status of churches. Deprived of tax exemption, many such institutions could not adjust quickly enough to survive. Religion did not die—no one can kill religion—nor did the government outlaw it. But the implied message, "keep your prayers to yourself," definitely got heard.

The Cloodys took down the sculpture of the angel. Sadly, no one knows what they did with it. In its place, they erected a sculpture of Jesus with his right arm upraised as if to deliver a blow. Because he looked down at the water in the fountain rather than out at passers-by, it was not clear what he intended to smite.

The Cloodys' method of training unbelievers was to make them live at first in bare rooms furnished with chamber pots and moldy mattresses, and do hard labor outside. As the unbelievers took the required steps on their faith journeys, they received benefits. A toilet. A sink. A chair. A place to wash their clothes. Shorter hours and easier tasks. At the end was the prize: a comfortable apartment with heat and air conditioning, a kitchen and a laundry, a new bed; and the right to profit from the labor of others.

One could almost pity them, this family who thought their money could buy anything. Almost. Some people said the Cloodys were driven mad with guilt over how their fortune was made. I will not repeat the story of where their family money came from. The dead are quiet now.

Toward the end, the Cloodys rounded up a few busloads of impoverished people and brought them to Cloodyville to be converted. *Those* people were grateful, though not for the reasons the Cloodys intended. They did what they had to do to stay. The preaching, the hours of back-breaking work, the heat of our summers, the snow and bitter cold of our winters—all were better than what they'd had before. Descendants of many of them live here still.

Except for those fortunate few, no one found a happy home in Cloodyville, not even the Cloodys themselves. Their training plan was, in the end, a failure. The incorrect Christians refused to be corrected. The unbelievers never showed up. The Cloodys found themselves presiding over boarded-up stores and empty homes.

By the time the Cloodys tried to sell out, Cloodyville had reduced the family fortune by one-third. Although family members still were obscenely wealthy by normal standards, the loss of all that money caused them to question their faith. Perhaps they did not have exclusive access to God after all.

The last thing the Cloodys did was tear down the large outdoor amphitheater that had stood since the early days of New Albion. They called it a money pit. Now there is an immense grassy verge down to the lake, and many undeparted ghosts.

One day, when our son Robin was five, he and I were walking by the place where the amphitheater used to be. He suddenly stopped dead because he said he saw a white-haired woman wearing a long white dress and carrying a big black case. He cried, "Mama, look!" but I saw nothing except my son's eyes tracking her as she walked up the road. He told me she disappeared at the door of the apartment house on Stone Street. That apartment house had been a hotel long ago.

We found out later that the big black case held a cello. The woman in the long white dress had played in the New Albion symphony; she could actually be identified from photographs. Her name was Desiree Long. Now she is a ghostly star.

Yes, our town is deeply haunted. The ghosts are from the old times. For them, it is perpetually high summer. Music plays and applause rings out over the lake. Some of us have heard the music and the applause, and even seen crowds sitting on the benches that are no longer there, their attention fixed on a stage that has long since gone to dust.

One ghost in an old house over on Dulci Street helps the family by cleaning and straightening things at night. They know her by the scent of lavender, winter and summer. They call her Lucy.

Destroying the heart of the town did not turn the Cloodys' fortune to sunshine. No one wanted to buy what they were selling. The Cloody-owned houses were run down from neglect and lack of occupancy. The holdouts who had not left New Albion when it became Cloodyville were, to put it mildly, uninterested in selling. From the point of view of potential buyers, this was unfortunate because the holdouts had the only nice houses left. Their responses to those would-be buyers have passed into local legend.

My ancestors Michaél and Sheilah Stillwater held out and held on. The years of hardship did not dim their love of the place. Sheilah once said to the Cloodys: "You will fail. We will watch." Both those things came to pass.

It was desperation that made the Cloodys do what they did next. They had only one serious offer for the slum that was supposed to have been their shining city. That offer came from a coven of witches who called themselves Cerridwen. Paganism had been ignored by the government because it was not considered to be a religion. As a result, paganism became more popular than it had been for a long time, although it would be an exaggeration to say that it caught on in a major way.

Certainly Cerridwen had wealthy silent partners, but to the end the witches stayed mum about who they were. There was no trail, either paper or electronic. The silent partners must have wanted their silence very badly. For a long time, rumors flew about the real source of the money behind Cerridwen. Atheists and agnostics whom the Cloodys had angered? Political enemies?

Corporate whiz-bangs who turned pagan when the sun went down? The government itself? The wretched Cloodys had to go back on everything they believed to sit down at the table with Cerridwen's leader, a vast woman who called herself Bronwyn Lowri. As she signed the necessary papers, her earrings chimed as if a breeze were blowing through them, though the room was airless and still.

When I imagine this scene, it is almost enough to make me believe that God has a sense of humor.

It hurt the Cloodys to admit that money mattered more to them than the principles of their fundamentalist faith, but they were going broke and Cloodyville was the reason. As they signed and felt sickened, the town stood placidly, in semi-ruin, awaiting its new name.

The coven considered naming the town Cerridwen after itself, but the example of Cloodyville was discouraging. After a long, angry debate between two factions, Cloodyville became Green Man. It almost became Hecate, but that name was rejected as obscure and lacking sex appeal. Cerridwen's ambition was to turn the village into a tourist attraction: gift shops, tarot readings, psychic healing, contacting the dead, spell-casting workshops, ghost walks, and communing with the natural world. Our town did provide ample opportunity to do those last two things.

With the aid of their mystery backers, the witches refurbished the hotel and rooming houses, turned houses into bed-and-breakfasts, and put gift shops where there had been boarded-up storefronts. They removed the sculpture of Jesus from the town fountain and replaced it with a great stone rectangle that wore the face of a man with vines and branches sprouting from his nose and mouth. The members of Cerriwiden who had favored Hecate hoped that tourists would not quite know what it was.

I've seen pictures of the Green Man sculpture. I assume the man was not supposed to look like a corpse, but he did.

The Cerriwidens pottered forward with their plans, although the tourism never amounted to as much as they wanted. "We can do all that in Networld" was a typical complaint against the enterprise. The fountain sculpture became riddled with cracks during a particularly cold winter and had to be thrown away. The witches lasted only half as long as the Cloodys did.

As the coven slowly sold off its holdings, the town began to recover something of its old identity. It took on the reputation of a rare and long-neglected work of art passed from one set of persons to another without anyone seeing its real value. Not true. For more than three hundred years, plenty of its people have known its real value.

No one wanted to change the name again. It is an awful pain to do this, and poor New Albion had already undergone the process twice. But we were no pagan community, and Green Man was all wrong. After some debate, the new settlers named the town for the fourth time. They named it Stillwater. The namers wrote, "Our town has survived war, fundamentalism, paganism, tourism, and e-beasts. Garvis Stillwater built better than he knew."

My eyes well with tears when I think of that kind and generous act. Perhaps Garvis Stillwater haunts the place, though I have never seen him. Ever since that momentous day in 2118, our fortunes have risen. We've become popular and hard to get into.

Some new residents moved here to hide from the Middle Machine Age with its domination by e-beasts who hate the human race. No one really hides anywhere, of course. However, we are law-abiding and our town is considered inconsequential in the grand scheme of things, so we are mostly left alone. In 2199 in the Reunited States there are supposed to be two classes of citizens: wealthy and poor in their separate silos. We walk a third path.

Some people fell in love with Star Lake. People whose churches had fallen found a safe haven to pray and meet in small groups in the physical world. People who make things—such as carpenters, artisans, musicians, and painters—found community. The town grew busy again. Musicians take the stage at our little concert hall. We repaired the roads, we rehabilitated the buildings. The fountain began to run again, although there is no sculpture in the center anymore.

Our town has facets. From some angles, it looks wealthy. From others, it does not. There are fewer single-family homes than there appear to be. Most houses are cut up into apartments, where people live comfortably but without luxuries. There are twelve apartment buildings, both condo and rental. All are former bed-and-breakfasts, hotels, and rooming houses.

However, living here has its price. People who move into Stillwater have to understand that. We do not live in silos, isolated from each other. We also are a true democracy, which requires charity, compromise, and superhuman tolerance for discussion. During our community meetings, democracy can seem like the most tiresome thing man ever invented. Everyone's opinion is weighed, and everyone has an opinion. Let that reality sink in.

In the Reunited States as a whole, Democracy exists in name only. People vote, or I should say "vote."

At birth, everyone begins to accumulate a Net profile called a ubot. A ubot is you in Networld. After sixteen years, ubots get voting rights, which means they are polled by govbots twice a year. The results of these polls are valuable to businesses. They are bought and sold openly around the world.

The results of ubot elections always indicate that everything is fine. "All right by me," say our ubots year after year. Here is the creed all Middle Machine Age children, including ours, are taught:

Your ubot is a chain forged link by link by your own actions.
You can no more alter the ubot than alter the past.

Our children also have to be taught the fiction that ubots cannot contain any errors. We teach them this because like you, we want to survive. The e-beasts destroyed an entire country, peaceful little Kartan, to make a point about power. That could have been us. That could have been anyone. We do as we are told, but not *just* what we are told. Outside the gates, our ubots say everything is fine. Inside the gates, people vote for themselves.

Who lives here? Everyone. Stillwater has—and has had for a long time—its own water treatment, sewage, and power plants. The people who work in those essential industries live here. So do the ones who repair the homes and systems, haul and recycle the trash, and maintain the roads. We are very close to self-sufficient.

Here is a thing: We pay for our utilities collectively, according to our ability. Nobody in Stillwater ever gets a bill for electricity or water, or anything like that. This reinforces a truth conveniently forgotten elsewhere: no one succeeds, or even survives, entirely by his own efforts.

Do you think trash collectors deserve less than a living wage? Try doing without them, my friend!

In 2129, I took the family home as the lion's share of my inheritance. That was seventy years ago. Since then, I have never lived anywhere else, or wanted to.

My brothers snickered. The Reunited States was going through another economic depression in 2129. Home values were falling almost hourly. Rose in Bloom was run down because the Stillwaters had not used it since before I was born. (At that point, the clan lived far away.) I think my choice proved to them what they had long suspected: that I am mentally aberrant in a way not measurable by conventional testing.

What my brothers did not know—and would not have believed—was that when I stepped across the threshold into the living room that smelt of mice and mildew, I fell to my knees and wept with gratitude. I had never been in love before and felt as if I were being carried aloft by a kite.

My soul grew and bloomed. Two years later, I married Josh Mackay. He owned a thriving nursery business never much troubled by hard times. People made pilgrimages to Mackay Gardens as if the place were sacred ground. Unlike me, he was a shrewd money manager. He knew what investments to put in his portfolio and what products to put on his shelves.

None of my relatives could believe this turn of events. Josh Mackay was a winner. By their lights, I was the opposite. I did not even have beauty to recommend me. In my twenties, I was a large girl with rough red skin and flyaway straw-colored hair. I was clumsy and shy. I had no interest in becoming more wealthy than I already was.

At my wedding, my brothers called me lucky to my face. They could not bring themselves to congratulate Josh even out of politeness, but Josh was the one who always said he could not believe his good fortune.

Eighteen months later, I gave birth to our first child, a boy we named Robin. He was healthy and strong. Will and Scarlett followed, also healthy and strong. Scarlett is our penalty child; in the Reunited States, there are heavy financial consequences for having more than two. We found this circumstance irritating the way a mosquito is irritating, but otherwise we did not care. At tax time, we swatted the Reunited States with a wad of money and moved on.

Now our penalty child runs Mackay Gardens, assisted by her husband and son. Now I am mother-in-law to Colm, grandmother to Paul, and great-grandmother to Jessie and Ulee. Strange to think that Scarlett's life is well past the halfway point, when I can still remember her one hour old.

I do not think my brothers died happy. Although they bought and sold with feverish intent to strike it rich, none of their investments proved to be geese that laid golden eggs. On the other hand, my bad joke of a house is now worth a small fortune. That fact annoyed them to the end.

It is so very beautiful here. Porches almost touch, and bicycles are common. Summer tourists come to gawk at what they call our quaintness, but no one who lives here would describe our town that way. "Quaint" is a belittling word. Our town is mighty.

But new troubles are on us now. Their source is a girl who was raised here, Kedzie Greer. Last year, she left town with a man named Jon Furey, who founded the Øutsider movement. With him, the Øutsider movement was clownish. With Kedzie, it is dangerous. Dangerous, I mean, to our tottering government.

The girl can call down lightning with her very presence. When she speaks, it is as if electric currents hum through the audience. She tells people that they have souls and makes them believe it. She tells them they can choose to live another way. Some have found to their astonishment that she is right.

Because our governors hate and fear this eighteen-year-old with the light around her, they hate and fear the place that formed her. In Networld, the filthiest screeds have been posted about Stillwater, where once there were gentle images of trees and sky and happiness. Some residents have been threatened and slandered just for living here. Julia Margoles and Adele Freyer, who adopted Kedzie as an infant, have been particularly popular victims. Without moving from your comfortable room or revealing your identity, you can rip someone to pieces. You can tell all the lies you want. It is obvious that many people no longer care about the difference between lies and truth.

Well-paid Networld commentators mock Stillwater for being wealthy, although most residents live in old apartments and work far harder than the average Networld commentator, I would think. It is true that our homes are worth a great deal of money now, but consider the reason: a lot of people want to move into Stillwater, but almost no one wants to move out. Real estate transactions are rare.

Here is one example close to me: My sons Robin and Will moved away from Stillwater and had some success in the world. Now they want to move back. They cannot get in, and it is not a matter of money. Nothing is available. They are looking elsewhere around the lake. Rose in Bloom will belong to all three of my children, and they can use it as they will, but no one child will live in it all year at the expense of the others.

Networld commentators mock us for our self-sufficiency in growing fruits and vegetables, which they call snobbery. How is it snobbish to plant a garden? I wonder. The minutes of our tedious community meetings in the name of democracy are published and sneered at.

Life in 2199 is cruel, but when was it not? I read histories for the perspective they provide and it used to be far, far worse than it is now. People died martyrs' deaths for believing in the wrong religion, which became the right religion a generation or two later. One survived by keeping one's opinions to oneself and covering the real self with an armor of lies. No wonder people feel sick to have their privacy violated, even in 2199, when everyone knows there is no such thing as privacy. The ability to keep secrets is a survival skill and always has been.

A lot of things are being said about our native daughter. Religiously inclined people say she is inspired by God like the saints of the past. People who dismiss all nonconformity as mental illness say she is schizophrenic. Cynics say she is a naïve girl being manipulated by Jon Furey. Depressives say she is a liar.

I think all the theories are far shy of truth. I think the truth is actually simple:

Kedzie wants everyone to live as we do here.

She grew up in this town, after all. She knows the place is real. When she got out in the world and saw people living in horrible ways, she felt compelled to point out their right to choose other ways to live. Brave girl.

I wonder what will happen next. I hope our town does not need to be renamed yet another time.

A week after Josh died (or as a neighbor put it, "was translated"), I was surprised to see him sitting in his favorite chair in the living room. This was no pale wraith. Josh wore his favorite blue and green plaid shirt. In the afterlife, he had good color and appeared vigorous.

I ran to him and touched his shoulder. He felt young and strong; the shock of it nearly knocked me down.

"There's nothing to this, Cassie," he said. "Nothing at all."

That first year of my widowhood, I often felt a presence standing beside me, or a cool hand on my brow. (I told you this town is haunted. The ghosts want to stay undeparted.) I could never be afraid. There is no reason to fear Josh in any world where you might meet him. The visits gradually grew less frequent and stopped entirely three years ago, but I believe that when my time comes I will see Josh again.

~ * ~

Life was made of vanishings. The people Cassie saw out her windows would cease to walk about. The ancient trees would come down. At some inconceivable future point, even Star Lake might boil into nothingness. Tenderness washed over Cassie as she thought of the people and things she loved. So many. She wanted to hold onto everything and everyone. She wanted to read to her great-grandchildren. She wanted to hear some dirty old blues. She wanted to eat salted caramel ice cream. She wanted to see Josh again. "I told you there was nothing to this, Cassie." At first she did not look. But it was Josh, whom she never had denied. She thought distantly, I can count the breaths I have left on my fingers. On the fingers of one hand, I can count them. Josh took her hands in his. His touch was real.

2

Leaving Home

June dawns, July noons, August evenings over, finished, done.
—Ray Bradbury, *Dandelion Wine*

In the end, it was the town gates that got to Kedzie. The gates were symbols of the caged feeling that was driving her crazy, and the fact that they had stood for hundreds of years was particularly maddening. Except for the summer tourists who came to gawk at what they called its quaintness, no one new ever showed up in Stillwater. Everybody who was already there knew everybody else who was already there. She could not walk past those heavy ironwork gates without wanting to shake them and cry out.

The vigilbots that manned the gates were polite and amiable. They said hello and wished you Godspeed. Although in 2199 vigilbots could be legally programmed to kill, the worst the Stillwater bots could do was surround people and deliver mild, persistent electric shocks. This, too, exasperated Kedzie. Why bother having a defense if it did not actually defend you?

Kedzie had ridden her bicycle over every street in Stillwater. She had been inside most of the houses. She had been to every community celebration: Christmas/Yule, Thanksgiving, Halloween, the first day of spring, summer, fall, winter. She had been to every picnic, done every volunteer job. Every step she took, she had taken before.

All the shopkeepers said, "Hi, Kedzie," when she entered. Kind Mr. Glimm always gave her a piece of candy, not caring to notice that she was an adult of sixteen. In the Reunited States in 2199, sixteen-year-olds were economically accountable for themselves. They had no legal right to be supported by anyone. Kedzie was so well-loved that it never occurred to her that one of the consequences of turning sixteen was that her parents could *force* her out. All she knew was that if she wanted to leave, her parents had no legal power to make her stay.

Kedzie's parents, Julia Margoles and Adele Freyer, practiced white witchcraft. As faithfully as any believers of old, they celebrated the Sabbats, they prayed to the God and Goddess. They did no harm to any creature on Earth. Kedzie had heard them say many times that they lived in harmony with "the great round"—the turning earth and the tenets of their faith.

It was fortunate that they never pressured Kedzie to adopt their beliefs, because she did not believe in anything they said or did. The idea of devoting her life to benign witchcraft—home, community, nature, and smiling—made her itch and toss restlessly in bed. She did not see what was so great about those elaborate stories her parents called spells:

Now walk into the forest. In a clearing, you will see a golden well with a bucket suspended from a rope. Lower the bucket into the well. All her parents' incantations sounded like that.

"We live in a false bubble," she said to her parents. "Stillwater is unreal."

Her mother Julia said that Stillwater was the real world. "Outside is the place of unreality," she said.

"It is not easy to live as we do," her mother Adele said. "We have to choose to do right every day of our lives, and it can be very, very tiresome. We do not always feel like it." She smiled as she said those words, but Kedzie did not smile back. Her mother was being irrelevant again. She strayed from the point every time she wanted to avoid facing something head-on. The habit had never irritated Kedzie more.

"How can you live so small?" Kedzie answered back. "We are what the tourists say we are, exotic animals in a zoo. We even live in a cage."

Adele had cried at those words. Julia flashed Kedzie an angry look. "You know nothing about evil, and in that way, we have failed you," she said. "You are naïve."

"If I am naïve, it is because you won't tell me things. You don't let me explore life outside these gates."

"You have a fine life here in Stillwater," Adele said.

Kedzie looked out the living room window, feeling like a prisoner peering out of a cell. The window was large and had diamond-shaped panes. As a small child she thought those diamonds made their house look like an enchanted cottage. Now the mullion shadows on the living room wall reminded her of bars. They blocked the light.

"If I don't get out soon, I'll run away," Kedzie said, sounding like the teenager she was. "I'll disappear off the face of the earth." She glared at her parents and stood with her arms crossed defiantly. When they refused to argue, she stormed out of the house.

Her parents watched her ride away on her pink and silver bike. More than anything else, that sight made them fear for her.

Her parents knew Stillwater public education was outmoded and eccentric. No Department of Education bureaucrat thought about Stillwater's public schooling at all, but if one ever did, he would place Stillwater's standards closer to those of the UnderWorld than those of the Outside. Julia and Adele had come face to face with a hard truth about their idyllic life in Stillwater: it had a price. It had left their daughter unprepared for anything else.

"UnderWorld kids have to go to work when they're my age," Kedzie said that night over dinner.

"And keep working until they die of it," Julia said. "That isn't you, Kedzie."

"Maybe it should be."

"Kedzie, you are young in ways those UnderWorld boys and girls are not. They grow up under harsh circumstances."

"Perhaps some more education," Adele offered timidly.

"I don't want go to school," Kedzie said. "No! I won't listen to any more reasons to stay." For the second time that day, she walked out, slamming the screen door with a bang. Again they watched her ride away on that pink and silver bike. Standing on their wide porch on that warm and beautiful night, surrounded by blooming plants in colorful pots, they felt both angry and afraid. They wanted to enjoy the summer as they had when Kedzie was little. Stillwater had been paradise then.

Kedzie rode to the lake, then parked her bike and walked up and down the shore, trying to cool down. Her parents thought she could not cope with life outside the gates. If she tried, she would quickly be defeated and run home, to live out her days in Stillwater and pass on the town's legacy to her children. They wanted this for her.

"No!" Kedzie cried to Star Lake. The waves slapped hard against the shoreline. The rough water answered that roughness is life. She imagined the lake still and stagnant, choked with weeds. It would not be at peace. It would be dying.

The waves washed a large dead muskellunge toward her. Its empty eyes told her nothing. Maybe its time had come, that was all. She tossed her head and walked away. Once again, she rode her bike around town. She could have done it blindfolded. She leaned the bike against an old sycamore tree and sat down in its shade. It had been her wise wishing tree when she was a little girl. Though she would admit it to no one, she talked to the tree still. "Tell me who I am supposed to be," she said to the vast gentle spirit residing within its trunk, branches, and leaves. "Show me the way."

The answer she got was the one she began with: a violent urge to leave Stillwater. But this time, when she felt it, she realized she did not entirely want it. She wanted to be told by someone—not her parents—that it was all right to stay home. How sweet it would be to stay forever loved. If she hung around for another year, Liam Ralston would propose to her. She was sure of it. She had so much. Why did she want to leave it all behind?

That question was not answered by God, Goddess, angels, or the wise wishing tree. Implacable, they only pointed out.

That night, Julia and Adele went to bed early to avoid confronting Kedzie when she returned. They had seen her through the tears and tantrums of babyhood, but this red anger was new. It burned. They had never deliberately avoided her before.

"Why won't she just take some more schooling?" Julia's lips were set in a hard line, as though she were preventing herself from saying a great many other things.

"When we moved here, we found the best place in the Reunited States," Adele said. "If Kedzie leaves, that is not what she going to find."

"I hate the law that says sixteen-year-olds are adults," Julia said. "Teenagers get tempted into the first lousy job they find. And why not? At that age, they think they are up for anything, and immortal besides. Then they discover three things: they can be broken, they are going to die like everyone else, and they have that lousy job for life."

"That won't be Kedzie," Adele said. "She can always come back here."

"We know what she thinks of staying in Stillwater," Julia snapped.

"Be fair, Julia. If she stayed, what would she do with herself? You know as well as I do that there are not many jobs."

"That's why she needs more education. That law is the devil."

At seven the next morning, Julia stumbled down to the kitchen, dressed in a faded gray T-shirt and beige linen trousers. Adele followed a few minutes later, wearing an old, unraveling white bathrobe marked for the rag bag. There was a great big hole under one arm. Julia sliced large pieces of chocolate cake for each of them. Adele put the coffee on. It was craven to eat for comfort, but neither felt brave that morning.

That was how Kedzie found them. She wore baggy red pajama bottoms and a little white top. She got herself a piece of cake.

"Where did you go last night?" Julia asked, though she and Adele usually never asked that question. They trusted their daughter. At least, they trusted the girl who was supposed to get some advanced education that permitted telecommuting and who would then stay in Stillwater forever.

"I was out walking and riding my bike, and thinking. No, I didn't decide to stay in Stillwater forever the way you want."

"Kedzie, don't act like such a child," Julia said.

"Don't treat me like one."

Kedzie and her parents ate in prickly silence from that point onward. Julia and Adele told themselves that when Kedzie started looking, she would find out quickly enough what kind of low-level job she could get with her standard education. She was intelligent; she would not put up with that. Kedzie made up her mind to find a job before the week was out.

Kedzie finished her cake and coffee and took the dishes to the sink to wash them. (She was a good girl; she did not walk away from dirty dishes.) She longed to be told that she was right in wanting to leave.

"We know what it's like to want another life," Adele said softly. Kedzie's eyes lit up; her mother understood! Julia glanced angrily at Adele.

"You don't know what you are talking about," Julia snapped.

"I just want to see some life outside Stillwater," Kedzie said. That was not true. She could not put into words the depths of her longing.

"You are too young to be on your own," Julia said.

"In Stillwater, I would be a store clerk," Kedzie said in an *I am a grownup* tone of voice that made her parents wince. "When my friend Annie married Weland, they moved into his old room in his parents' house because they had nowhere else to go. How would you like that?"

"There is no room in this little house," Adele said, evading the question the way she did when confronted with something unpleasant. "But you need a plan beyond just getting out."

"There is another thing," Julia said. "You won't get a better job outside the gates. You would still be a clerk or something like that. The difference would be that you would not have a home."

At that, Kedzie flounced upstairs to research possible jobs. For hours, intense silence emanated from her bedroom. Kedzie browsed dozens of career sites, job sites, and educational websites. She did not want anything they were pitching. She went to Stillwater's website. It was meant to make the town appear beautiful and magical, but to Kedzie's jaded eyes, the website just looked dull. She took a sugar hit from a candy bar and kept cruising. Nothing.

Kedzie could not sleep that night. Even the soporific effect of her parents' spells could not make her close her eyes. At three in the morning, she once again went cruising in Networld. What if she found the right job? What if she didn't? Her heart pounded with excitement and dread.

She browsed career, job, and educational websites until her eyes were bloodshot and her vision blurred. Something was out there. It had to be. The candy bar wrappers piled up. Kedzie's nerves were scratched and raw.

Then at a quarter to five in the morning, she found work she wanted. The job appeared on the screen suddenly, clothed in glory. Kedzie applied on the spot. She had no experience, but that would not eliminate her from consideration if this job was truly hers. The company that was hiring would know it belonged to her, wouldn't they? Surely they would.

It was light when Kedzie crashed into sleep and early afternoon when she opened her eyes. Her first emotion was terror that the job had been a dream, that there was no job. There was a sour taste in her mouth, and her stomach was uneasy. She rolled over in bed and checked her email.

There was an answer.

"Read it," she whispered to her mobile. It obliged.

"We are pleased to offer you the job of Comforter at HW44. Details to follow."

Adele and Julia knew from the minute Kedzie walked downstairs that something was up. They made cups of tea and sat at the kitchen table with their daughter, watching her fidget. After putting spoonful after spoonful of sugar into a cup of coffee, Kedzie set it aside without tasting it. She got a package of plain crackers from the pantry and munched them one by one.

Finally she said to her parents, "I found a job I want. Outside the gates."

"We think you need more education," Adele said. She stared into her cup of tea as if it had something to tell her.

"In the UnderWorld, someone my age goes to work for life."

"Which is very sad," Julia said. She was supposed to be the strong one, Adele the soft. But Julia was the one who began to cry.

"Stop acting as if I am going to die," Kedzie said. Sugar, broken sleep, excitement, and terror roared inside her like a cage of hungry tigers. She must give details. Once she named the job, she knew she would have to be prepared to defend it. After wavering for a few seconds, she plunged into her spiel as she might diving into the coldest depths of Star Lake.

"A place not far from here is looking to hire Comforters. In Networld I saw an ad: free room and board, patient contact, and a chance to matter."

"A chance to matter," she repeated.

"What is the name of this place and what are Comforters?" Julia asked.

"The place is called HW44," Kedzie said, hoping her parents did not know what the initials stood for. But they did know. Kedzie could tell from their dismayed expressions and the way Adele set her mug of tea down with a bang.

"A *human warehouse?*" Adele cried. "Oh no, Kedzie. Oh no."

In the meantime, Julia was already in Networld doing research. Her mobile blinked as it scavenged for information about human warehouses, the ads they ran, and what people said about working in such places. Kedzie did not like the frown lines on her mother's face.

"Do you know the purpose of human warehouses?" Julia demanded.

"HWs," Kedzie mumbled.

"Don't you dare use those lying initials," Adele said. Kedzie looked up, shocked. Neither of her parents had never spoken to her in that tone before.

"Imagine a place so awful that the government doesn't even try to give it a pretty name," Julia said. "Imagine a place where all they let you know is the stark initials of it, 'HW.' "

"People's lives are hard enough when they are healthy and employed," Adele said. "How do you think they are treated when they can't work?"

"The warehouses hire Comforters—that tells me they do care about people," Kedzie cried.

"That is not what it tells me," Adele said. "I think to call this job 'Comforter' is merely another lie."

"The accommodations are nice," Kedzie continued, eager to please her parents. "We get apartments, not rooms, and they come with a TV and a mobile, and all the furnishings. We even get garden space." She leaned forward across the kitchen table, wanting them to share her excitement. Her eyes were bright.

"I wonder why they provide room and board," said Adele. "It is not a typical thing to do. Maybe they don't want warehouse workers mingling with other people."

"There is Networld!" Kedzie said. "Anybody can share anything they like, no matter where they are."

Kedzie knew as well as her parents did that this was not true. Her cheeks reddened.

"We raised you to be smarter than that, Kedzie," Adele said.

"The employees in HWs have nothing to say," Julia said, frowning at her mobile. "Not one word in all the depth and breadth of Networld is from a worker in a human warehouse. At least none that are identified as such."

"The people in those places need help." Kedzie remained defiant.

Julia drew a deep breath, as if to calm herself. "We will all sleep on it," she said in a tone of forced reasonableness.

"I already accepted their job offer," Kedzie said. "I am going."

"A small pause for thought before your life changes irrevocably and forever might be a good idea," Julia said. Her sarcasm was withering and absolute.

"You didn't hesitate that winter night when you took me in."

"We told you that story so many times," Adele said. "Now you want to take a leap of faith, too." She slumped against Julia, though Julia was shorter than she was. High color was in Julia's cheeks. Unspoken in both their minds was this thought: This thing been waiting to happen ever since the night they found infant Kedzie abandoned in a basket on their front porch. Their daughter was destined to deny that she belonged with them.

"How will you get there?" Julia said. "You don't drive and neither do we."

"I'll find a way," Kedzie said stubbornly. She retreated to her room and checked the cost of a car service from Stillwater to HW44. The price made her sick. Her parents would not pay it. No one would. She would have to think of something else.

She texted every friend she had because she did not want to stay alone with her nervousness and excitement. No one sent her a big smile or said, "All right!" However, Ella, Val, Lucinda, and Blake agreed to meet her by the lake at seven that night. She told her parents, "I won't be here for dinner."

Julia said, "As you wish. We will talk tomorrow."

Kedzie texted her friends: "Bring beer. Lots of beer."

At the Stillwater grocery store, Kedzie did not have enough money to pay for the bags of chips and pretzels she wanted. The owner, Mr. Forester, said he trusted her. He had known her since she was a baby. (Of course he did. Every last bleeding person in Stillwater had known her since was a baby.) He put the snacks in a bag and, smiling, added a candy bar. She ate it sitting by herself at a table in the community center, very pointedly not thinking of the delicious dinner she could have at home.

Kedzie, Ella, Val, Lucinda, and Blake convened a seminar on life that night. They sipped beer and pondered the future as deeply as they knew how, while the day grew dimmer and the stars brighter. Star Lake was calm. Kedzie told them her plans. In their faces she saw understanding about why she wanted to get out of Stillwater but none whatsoever about her choice of employer.

"You don't even know what it means to have a job," Blake said to Kedzie. He had been employed as an assistant groundskeeper since the age of twelve and now had an entry-level position at Mackay Gardens, a plum job if you didn't mind hard outdoor work. Blake did not mind it.

"I want to know what it means," Kedzie said. She ran a finger lightly up and down the side of her beer bottle. She looked no one in the eye.

"We know how you feel, wanting to escape," Val said. "I mean to get out as soon as I get my Associate Networking degree. I can get a job Outside, move to the big city. I think I can." His voice faded into silence.

"Cities aren't anything special," Ella said. "I've been to Empre St York seven times. You can have it."

"I go into virtual reality five, six hours a week," Val said. "I see the world."

"My parents won't allow a virtual reality simulator in the house," Kedzie said.

Her friends smiled at her stilted choice of words. Everyone else just said VR.

"You spend enough time in VR at my house," Ella said.

"Long ago, a hundred thousand people came through Stillwater every summer," Val said. "It was called New Albion then."

Idle nods went round in the twilight.

"You can take a virtual tour of Stillwater," Ella said. "I did it once. It looks pretty."

"That's how tourism works now," Blake said. "When you take a virtual tour, the place you are touring gets a royalty."

"Simple and easy," Lucinda said, yawning. Of the five, she came from the wealthiest family. She was slender and beautiful, and looked like the ballet dancer she was.

"Being there matters," Blake said. "People can order stuff online and take virtual tours of Mackay Gardens, but every spring we get crowds for real. It is not the same experience in VR."

Ella shrugged. "Better, I think," she said.

"No," Blake said. "Not better at all."

"There's another thing about leaving home," Val said. "There isn't much work around here and no place to live unless we want to stay with our parents for the rest of our lives."

"When Annie married Weland, they had nowhere to go. They live in his old room," Kedzie said.

The five of them shook their heads sadly. How would Annie and Weland survive, their lives so dire right from the start?

"Nothing becomes available in Stillwater unless someone dies, and that's a fact," Val said.

"The other towns around Star Lake are the same."

"I wish someone would build some apartments."

"My father says Stillwater can't grow because it would be illegal to expand its boundaries."

"Somewhere else then."

"No one around here *wants* their towns to grow. That's why we either have to get out or live with our parents for the rest of our lives. "

Ella was quiet for a minute or so, sipping her beer. Then she looked Kedzie in the eye. "Why do you want a job like that?" she asked.

Kedzie shook her head. "I just know I do," she said.

For another forty minutes or so, the five sixteen-year-olds drifted with their thoughts. Beers were cracked open. Chips and pretzels were crunched. Finally Val said he had to be going.

Lucinda, who seemed bored, agreed at once that it was time to leave. Blake offered to walk her home.

Only Kedzie and Ella remained at the picnic table under the Milky Way. A fish leapt out of the water somewhere in the dark.

"I wish you weren't going away," Ella said.

"That's what my parents say."

"I get it, though. There are no good jobs for us unless we get advanced degrees," Ella said sadly. "I hate school."

That her parents had said much the same thing annoyed Kedzie, not because she thought they were lying but because she thought they underestimated her ability to rise above her circumstances. She would spin gold at HW44.

She drank the rest of her beer. Ella did the same. Both put their bottles in the recycling bin. No good Stillwater kid forgot about recycling, not even when that kid was a little drunk.

They noticed something strange, not explained by the beer: there were lights over the water, twinkling like snowflakes. It was a dazzling, delicate show, as beautiful as the first snowfall in winter, except that nothing fell. Black and inscrutable, the lake lapped at the shore.

The lights shaped themselves into almost-human creatures dancing over the water. Kedzie and Ella watched the graceful movements of the creatures in midair and their reflections in the water.

"Do you see that?" Kedzie asked Ella.

"Yes," Ella said. "Oh, it is beautiful."

"What is it?" Kedzie said, though she knew the answer: Stillwater had many ghostly inhabitants, and everyone saw them eventually.

"Maybe the spirits of people who drowned in Star Lake. Look how happy they are now."

A crazy thought burst into Kedzie's mind. "Even the dead can't get away from Stillwater," she said. "You don't live here till you die. You live here forever."

She turned and fled from the vision. Ella had to follow as if she were a little kid trying to keep up with an older sister. Kedzie did not stop until she saw the golden lights on her porch at 12 Geranium Lane. Her parents were there, rocking silently.

Her parents the witches.

Ella caught up to her. "Why did you run away?" she demanded.

"I got scared," Kedzie whispered. "Don't talk about it."

"It was just ghosts," Ella said.

"Don't tell anyone."

"Nobody will think I'm crazy if I tell," Ella said.

"No," Kedzie said. "I don't want to be one of those people who talks about ghosts."

"I'll wait till Halloween," Ella said.

"No!"

"You need to calm down," Ella said. "They don't want to hurt us." She went off into the night.

Both Kedzie's witch parents sat on the porch, just as she had left them. She stepped inside, pulled the screen door closed, and settled into a rocking chair, to rock and breathe until she felt calm again. She did not speak of the ghostly vision because it belonged to her, not to them. If she spoke of it, they would find a way to claim it for themselves. They might cast a spell and read runes, and every other weird thing they did. They would tell her what they found out. Kedzie did not want to know.

That night, lying side by side under a midnight blue quilt embellished with zodiac symbols in silver and a rising sun in gold, Julia and Adele talked to each other in reasonable tones. Kedzie believed she could not grow beyond childhood in Stillwater. They could not tell her she was wrong; she had to find that out for herself. When she did, she would return home and seek the advanced education she needed for a career.

She was wrong, but she would go out and be wrong with all her heart and all her mind and all her goodwill. They remembered how that felt. If they were honest with themselves, they understood why she was angry at them for trying to prevent it.

Both Julia and Adele had a strong sense of fair play—the ability to see both sides of a question, to suppress their own feelings in service of greater understanding. Their vow of doing no harm extended to refusing to impose their will on others. They would cast no spells to try to prevent Kedzie from going to work at a human warehouse. It was wrong to ask the spirit world for aid in preventing their daughter from doing something she had set her whole soul on doing.

"We could go scrying," Adele said. "That would not be interference."

Menaced by fears that reason and fair play had not entirely quieted, they yielded to the temptation to divine the future. They had not done so in many years.

Far back on a shelf in their bedroom closet was a black mirror on a bronze stand, covered by a large piece of blue silk. Adele unwrapped the mirror. Clasping it tightly in both hands, she carried it to a low table and set it precisely in the center. Together, Julia and Adele put twenty-one beeswax candles in a circle around the mirror and lit them. They created around themselves a circle of protection to ward off any evil spirits that might be about.

At first they saw nothing. Then a shape as beautiful as a snowflake began to form. At the moment it reached perfection, the snowflake burst apart. The delicate, beautiful pattern shattered before their eyes. What happened next was worse.

The mirror cracked and fell from the stand onto the floor in two jagged pieces. From the pieces rose a wisp of smoke. Julia and Adele exchanged horrified looks. The mirror had broken *before* it fell, not after. The message was clear: they had been trying to see something forbidden. Some terrible energy said, "Keep out."

All night they lay upon their bed wrapped in the quilt whose symbols seemed to carry a new charge of menace. At first light, Adele threw a blanket over the shards of mirror as gingerly as if she were trapping a bat. She carried the bundle outside and put it in a trash can. That morning, Kedzie bounced around, all smiles, and the late summer sun shone through the windows Adele had polished to brilliance that morning, making endless circles with her cloth. She kept polishing long after the glass was clean.

Kedzie drank a second cup of coffee and put on her jacket. She told them she was going to ask all her friends' parents in person whether they could give her a ride to HW44. Julia and Adele knew that the effort would be fruitless. HW44 was located in the general vicinity of a slummy UnderWorld town named ESY-Backland. Other than ESY-Backland, HW44 had no near neighbors of any kind. Nobody from Stillwater would be going that way.

"There is a shard of comfort," Julia said, "in knowing that she would not believe us about the scrying mirror anyway."

"A shard." Adele permitted herself a tiny smile.

"We know what she thinks of our witchcraft."

"Maybe nonbelievers are immune to the effects of the spirit world."

"Kedzie always laughed when we cast spells."

Both had the same thought: *Kedzie, keep laughing. Stay strong.*

"She would not forgive us if we refused to help her. Who knows what else would not forgive us."

The two women looked old and chilled. Operating on about two hours sleep between them, they called in a favor.

So it was that on June 29, 2199, Kedzie left Stillwater sitting in the well-upholstered back seat of Dr. Porter Magnim's black limousine, driven by a black-uniformed chauffeur. Dr. Magnim sat beside her, radiating resentment. It was slightly past seven in the morning. There was a strong breeze, a harbinger of storms.

In the trunk was her suitcase, a hand-me-down from her parents. On the floor between her feet was a cardboard box containing two tenderly nurtured plants her parents had dug up from their cottage garden and put in clay pots. One was a hosta, its deep green leaves edged with gold. The other was a perennial geranium, its large flowers delicately veined in violet and blue, its leaves cinnamon scented. "These are your leave-taking gifts,"

Adele said. "Care for them and think of us, caring for you. Remember to put the hosta in the shade." When the limo turned out of the gates of Stillwater, Kedzie looked back at the town, shining in the dawn like an ethereal jewel. It held all she knew so far of life, and she watched it grow smaller and smaller in the distance.

Dr. Magnim sat all the way over on his side of the back seat. His mobile absorbed all his attention. Kedzie fiddled with her own mobile, paging nervously through images she did not care about seeing and reading words that barely registered. Pockets of fear were forming in her mind. What if? What if?

Stronger than the fear, though, was the sense that something grown-up was finally happening to her. She had her first job. She was leaving home.

However, it was hard to feel like an adult while sitting in the back seat of Dr. Magnim's limo like a doll all dressed up and waiting for the grownups to deliver her to a birthday party. Dr. Magnim did not want to help Kedzie get where she wanted to go; he had barely said hello when he arrived with the limo at five that morning.

Kedzie closed her eyes, but she knew there would be no sleep for her, no matter how quiet the car or how smooth the ride. She texted her friend Ella but got no answer. She tried three more friends with the same result. Too early in the morning.

Within twenty-five minutes, Dr. Magnim arrived at his destination—the leafy campus of the Granding Institute for Artificial Intelligence, a think tank. He said goodbye. He did not say good luck. Kedzie and the chauffeur went on alone for three more hours. Her friends finally texted good luck, good wishes, good hunting. Ella said, "May the ghosts go with you."

"Thank you," Kedzie texted back with a smile.

"Got to go," Ella said. "Good luck."

The black car glided onward. "Do you like your job?" Kedzie asked the chauffeur. She was not trying to offend him, just making conversation, but she could tell by the way he stiffened his back that he was insulted. He pretended he did not hear her. Dr. Magnim had probably already forgotten she was ever in the car.

"How far now?" she asked the chauffeur. She would make him talk even if he didn't want to.

He replied in a bored monotone voice, "Maybe fifteen minutes."

They were getting close. Kedzie peered out the window, but there was nothing to see in this anonymous, stunted landscape; it was a blank. Even the sky seemed exhausted; its blue was weak, without character. Stillwater skies always seemed full of color and light—an effect, more than likely, of Star Lake.

The chauffeur turned up a narrow, unmarked road. Unhealthy trees leaned in for a better look at Dr. Magnim's elegant limousine as it glided toward HW44. The chauffeur had to pull over to the shoulder to make way for a white van with a strange double-decker construction. The windows of the van were dark; Kedzie could not make out any faces. For the first time, she felt an honest stab of terror, like a four-year-old scared of the dark.

Her parents used to let her sleep between them when she woke up frightened. Those days were gone. Whatever happened at HW44, they were not coming back.

The chauffeur stopped the limousine in front of a sand-colored building twelve stories high. Perhaps a quarter mile away was a second sand-colored building six stories high. Kedzie hesitated. "Is this the dormitory?" she asked.

"It's where HW44 is supposed to be," the chauffeur said. The back of his neck was dark with sweat and weariness.

"Thank you," Kedzie said. "I know it was a long trip."

"It wasn't your fault," the chauffeur said, somewhat mollified.

"What is your name?" Kedzie asked.

"Fruglé," the chauffeur said. "Emory Fruglé."

"Best of luck to you," Kedzie said.

"I hope you find what you're looking for," Fruglé said.

Carrying her suitcase, with the hosta and geranium in their cardboard box, Kedzie walked toward the tall building, moving slowly because her burdens were awkward to carry. There were stone steps and an opaque set of double doors that required Kedzie to set her possessions down and push hard against one to open it. Then, bracing the door against her hip, she dragged the suitcase and pushed the box into the reception area. It was empty except for one young man who sat behind a semicircular desk.

The young man was powerfully built, with a shaved head and a nose ring shaped like a bone. He was dressed in black. Chains dangled from his shirt. Metal studs marched down his pants. When she first saw him, Kedzie wanted to laugh. Instead, she walked up to the desk, gave her name, and announced that she had been hired to work at HW44. The young man watched her with cold eyes. "Your name is Jahn," she said, reading his ID badge.

"It is," he said, unsmiling. "And you are in the wrong place."

"What?"

"I saw you drive up in that big black car. Are you retarded or just insane?"

Kedzie's cheeks flushed.

"If you're so stupid that you want to stay here, go around back to the dormitory" Jahn said. "They'll assign you a room."

"But who?—"

"I got no information for you. Go to the back."

Kedzie picked up her suitcase and box of plants, and turned to leave. Over her shoulder she asked, "What do you do here?"

"I give directions to people too dumb to know they're lost," he said curtly.

"Lucky you," Kedzie said. She turned away, this time for good. She carried her things outside to find that the limousine was gone. She looked this way and that for signs of activity—Stillwater's streets were full of people at all hours of the day. Here she saw no one. HW44 stood behind her, all twelve stories utterly silent, even though she knew there had to be many people inside. It had begun to rain just a little. Kedzie felt the fatigue of a long morning spent in uncongenial company. She started along the path to the dormitory.

On the rough pavement, the wheels of the suitcase stuttered, then abruptly stopped turning. The rich soil from their garden was scattered all over the path, slowly turning into mud. Kedzie scooped the startled plants back into the box, which was itself moist and beginning to soften.

The entrance to the dormitory required her to punch in a visitor code, which she got wrong the first time. A squawking voice told her to open the door when she heard a click. There was a click, but she did not grab the door handle quickly enough. There was another squawk that probably meant, "Try again, fool."

Tensely, Kedzie held her hand just above the door handle and waited for the click. When it came, she grabbed the handle and pulled. To her relief, the door opened. She maneuvered the suitcase halfway through the door, then used it to prop the door open so she could bring in the plants.

Apparently the door found this behavior suspect, for it began to scream.

"That door doesn't work too well for visitors," said a woman sitting behind a desk in the lobby. Her voice was perfectly normal; the security system must have been responsible for the squawk. Kedzie wondered why. She hauled her suitcase through the screaming door and went up to the desk.

The woman was in her twenties, with straight brown hair and a plain but pleasant face. Her ID badge said her name was Mona Sadler. A tamper-proof identity cuff marked her as an inhabitant of the UnderWorld. When she saw Kedzie looking at the cuff, she lowered her eyes, apparently ashamed of her status. Her manner was quiet and withdrawn, yet friendly; she reminded Kedzie of a puppy that feared people but still yearned to be accepted by them.

"Your name?" Mona asked, still not meeting Kedzie's eyes.

"Kedzie Greer. I start work tomorrow as a Comforter."

Mona swiped Kedzie's ID card. "You are in room 214," she said, handing her a keycard. "Elevator is to the right." Kedzie thought Mona looked as though she wanted to say more, but the young woman did not continue.

Kedzie attempted to draw Mona out. "Are the apartments nice?" she asked.

Having been raised in Stillwater's close-knit community, Kedzie was attuned to human interactions. Otherwise, she would not have noticed how Mona flinched at her question.

"What do you think?" Mona said.

3

Julia and Adele

You'll live and get hurt," she said. "But when it's time, tell me. Say goodbye.
—Ray Bradbury, *Something Wicked This Way Comes*

On the porch of the little blue house at 12 Geranium Lane, Julia Margoles and Adele Freyer sat back in the shadows. Adele was tall and plump, with yellow hair she described as honey-colored and a rosy complexion. Julia was small and thin, with dark brown hair and eyes.

After a sleepless night, they had gotten up early to see their daughter Kedzie off on her journey to Human Warehouse 44. In the sleepy early morning, they had been the souls of reason. They understood why Kedzie wanted to test herself, they said. If it didn't work out she could come home, they said. Nothing ventured, nothing gained, they said.

That pompous jackass Dr. Porter Magnim owed them a favor. "Favor repaid," he said tersely when Kedzie got into his chauffeured limousine. He sat in the back seat of his pretentious machine as far away from their daughter as he could get. He was bound for the Granding Institute for Artificial Intelligence. Kedzie was going much further. As parents must do, Julia and Adele waved frantically as the chauffeur drove them away. In a minute, she was gone from them.

That was that. They stood on the sidewalk, suddenly alone.

"Once upon a time we thought we knew everything," Julia said to Adele sadly.

"We knew where we were going," Adele said.

"We cast off and sailed away," Julia said. "Then the compass and chart disappeared."

"Kedzie," Adele sighed. She reached for Julia's hand. They went back into the kitchen to drink coffee and give themselves over to memories. They had not sought parenthood. Parenthood sought them.

On the night before Yule sixteen years ago, they were drinking a bit of brandy after evening prayers. The fire was burning low. The rich aroma of cinnamon, nutmeg, and ginger drifted in from a batch of spice cookies cooling on the kitchen counter. They were at peace with themselves and the world—until they heard a small noise on the porch.

Because they lived in Stillwater, where there was nothing to fear, they threw capes over their shoulders and went outside. In a wicker basket was a baby, covered by a blue and white blanket. She had dark, silky hair, deep blue eyes, and a faint oriental cast to her features. The moon emerged from behind the clouds and shone on that basket as if it wanted to show how beautiful she was. Snow was falling very gently.

"Oh," Adele whispered. "How strange."

"And our bar for strangeness is set extraordinarily high," Julia said.

They both blinked, but neither of them expected the baby to disappear. This was no phantom child. They could see the baby's breath and their own breaths mingling in the cold air, as if their lives were already irrevocably intertwined. She lay in her basket and looked up at them, silently waiting.

For a long moment they did nothing but look at the swirling waltz of snow.

Adele picked up the basket but it felt awkward, about to tip over, so she set it down again. The baby began to cry. Working together, they managed to lift the basket and hold it steady. They each wondered, without needing to say it aloud: How could the mother have managed to carry such a heavy burden alone and undetected? Clasping it tightly against their bodies, using their hips as shelves, they maneuvered the basket into the house. Adele turned down the blanket and picked up the baby, who stopped crying at once.

The mother came from outside the Stillwater gates, of that they were certain. No one could keep a pregnancy completely secret in this town, nor would there have been any motive for concealment. This woman had abandoned her infant on the porch of strangers. Did she sense that her baby's destiny lay with them? Did she want to protect her? Did she just want to get rid of her?

Their old lives ended that winter night. When that baby smiled so innocently at them, she was committing, they came to believe, just the first of her many revolutionary acts.

They decided, without much discussion, to adopt her. For two weeks, they tried to choose a name but found none that made sense, either for them or for her. Baby books and biographical dictionaries were no help. Nothing fit the baby whose smile had sent them down a new road.

Then Adele had a vision while praying. When she visualized the forest glen where she went in her mind to find guidance and peace, she saw the name "Kedzie Greer" painted in gold on a white signpost. It was a good name for a heroine, Julia and Adele thought with joy and optimism. It did not dawn on them that a heroine's name might be an unwise choice.

On the day Kedzie left to do Goddess knows what, they wished they had named her Jean-Millie, and given her a tongue-stumbling hyphenated last name: Jean-Millie Margoles-Freyer. A girl with a name like that would still be safe at home with them.

They blundered through her childhood, making many mistakes. But children are stronger than adults; they can bear things that would split an adult in two. Julia and Adele applied themselves diligently to parenthood, learning and correcting their ways. Always in the back of their minds was cold fear that Kedzie's natural mother would return.

When Kedzie ate animal crackers and milk, the world was as wide as animal crackers and milk. When she didn't want to take a nap, her anger was red and hot and absolute. When she wanted to wear her footie pajamas, she brought them to one of her parents. This might be at bedtime, or it might be two in the afternoon. The world was as wide as those footie pajamas. If they failed in their duty to wriggle Kedzie into them, they would hear her loud complaints. With Kedzie, Julia and Adele's lives became slapdash, funny, and improvisational. The days were small as acorns with chores and duties, but they became wondrously wide when split open.

When Kedzie was very small, lake sunfish and perch would swim right into her hands. She would hold them for a moment in wonder.

Before that snowy night before Yule, Julia and Adele achieved success according to their plans. Inside and outside the gates of Stillwater, they were semi-famous, as much as any mere mortals can be in a world run by artificial intelligence and Networld e-beasts.

They arranged their days around plans and goals. Today I must write 2000 words. Today I must walk five miles for my health. Today I must rearrange the objects on the altar.

Their fame came from three books. The first one, *The White Lantern: Why Spirit Matters,* was a perennial best seller. Two others followed: *Soul Kitchen* and *Soul Rising.* They wrote *Soul Rising* after they became parents, but they were careful to avoid writing exclusively about parenthood. "There are a thousand ways for the soul to rise," they said, "and as many ways for it to wither."

Like many parents, they were afraid to send Kedzie to school. Would she thrive and prosper? Or would she wither unexpectedly, like a young plant in unsuitable conditions? But Kedzie in school made them proud.

The school, Stillwater Omni, stood squarely just where it has stood since 1911, on the corner of Revere and Water streets and within sight of the lake. It was the most visible marker of Stillwater's quaintness. Every summer, tourists stared at rooms decorated with students' artwork and odd, lumpy crafts of uncertain purpose. Because Stillwater Omni had Networld access like every other place in the Reunited States, tourists did not understand why the children were still herded together to learn. In

2199, young people did not receive lessons in the presence of each other. That had not been done, even in the UnderWorld, for many generations.

"We've found children do better when they are not physically alone," the docents explained patiently. "And they love to play on the grounds." The tourists snapped photos of the penknife-scarred desks in the small school rooms, the displays of the

arts and crafts fashioned by students. After a few minutes passed and the tourists finished taking pictures, they were ready to be led to the next odd site in Stillwater.

Kedzie's leadership role seemed to be waiting for her on the first day she walked into Stillwater Omni. This role did not change over time. From the little girl who decided what games to play during recess to the young teenager who directed and starred in the school play (that creaking antique, Our Town), Kedzie ruled without cruelty or malice. She ruled without effort. Such natural authority was foreign to Julia and Adele. Even when they held workshops for their faithful readers, covering subjects such as dark green religion and care of the soul, they let participants steer the agendas. They were the gentlest of witches.

One spring day when she was nine, Kedzie came home from school in tears, with her right hand cut and bruised. Her face was crumpled with sadness. She stumbled upstairs without telling her parents anything, nor did she say what happened until that evening. By that time, careful tending of the injured hand and a good dinner had mollified her a little. Adele made her a sling out of a red kerchief.

Kedzie said she had picked an overweight boy named Morris Slater for her kickball team. Rather than giving her the big smile she expected, he hung back and looked at the ground. He told her to go to hell.

Safe in her own living room, she crossed her arms in front of her chest, something she always did she felt threatened. She must have crossed her arms the same way when Morris Slater hurled his unhappy words in her face.

"He said I didn't really want him on my team, but I did."

The cruelty of the situation was that she *did* want Morris Slater on her team. Her attitude was to Julia and Adele's credit, or entirely their fault, depending on how you looked at it. They'd taught her a way seeing people as essences—you could understand a person's essence in a second if you used the powers of finely honed sensitivity and perception. She wanted the souls of the unpopular ones to burn a little more brightly. She was not absolutely sure that picking an unpopular kid first would fan those flames, but she thought it might.

"Morris said he couldn't play kickball because he wore special shoes. They were brown and ugly."

"Maybe that is true," Julia said.

"I saw a worm on the pavement," Kedzie said. Her eyes brimmed with tears.

This comment was bewildering. "Do you mean that you thought of Morris like you think of the worms you rescue after a rainstorm?" Adele asked.

"No!" Kedzie said. "I reached down to rescue a real worm, not Morris Slater. He stamped on my hand, then he stamped on the worm, then he ran away."

"That was wrong of him."

"I know!" cried Kedzie. "Now the worm is dead, and Morris Slater will never be on a kickball team, not mine or anyone else's."

Julia and Adele said that Morris Slater probably didn't want to play sports.

"I don't understand," Kedzie said sadly. "Why didn't he want to be helped? Didn't he want to shine?"

They said that some people can't be helped by any force in this world or any other. This is why some people murder heroes, because heroes remind them of a bright, shining light that they will never know themselves. Kedzie looked at them for a long time, with her bruised hand in a homemade sling.

Julia and Adele felt like fools—or worse than fools. Armed with their high idealism, Kedzie had been hurt and humiliated that spring day. They feared she was heading for far worse than that.

Julia repeated what they had been telling themselves nonstop for weeks: Kedzie leaving home was not the end of the world. The summer sun in all its innocence poured through the diamond-paned living room window, as if this were a glorious day.

"The mirror cracked from side to side," Adele said. The memory of the dreadful night when they used the scrying mirror to see into the future came back to both of them.

"We don't know what that means," Julia said.

"Yes, we do."

"No," Julia said. "You are led too easily, Adele. We may have just scared ourselves like children at Halloween. We were already upset."

"That wasn't how you were talking at the time. You were as frightened as I."

"We couldn't legally do anything to make Kedzie stay at home," Julia said wearily.

"We could have done plenty of other things to make Kedzie stay at home. If we had made the usual arguments, she would have listened. But we didn't. Oh God, we didn't."

"Adele, stop talking tragedy. You always exaggerate." Julia got up and poured herself another cup of coffee. She added an uncharacteristically large amount of cream and sugar.

"I am going to call the coven to a meeting," Adele said.

"The coven is four other solitary practitioners," Julia snapped. "Most of the time all we do is exchange recipes."

"Except for Menjou," Adele said. Her voice was soft and tired. "Menjou is a brilliant success in Networld, casting spells and giving advice."

"She's a good person, at least," Julia said. "She wouldn't hurt anyone no matter how much they paid her."

"Lucky for the world that she wouldn't," Adele said. "Menjou could do a lot of damage."

The Stillwater witches, Clarissa, Menjou, Farelle, and Toni, agreed to come to the house at seven that evening. All afternoon, Adele alternately fussed with the altar, knelt in prayer, listened to the music, and fidgeted in the kitchen. Julia went for a walk, came back, and went out again. She got increasingly irritated, a feeling she tried to suppress.

"Kedzie doesn't believe," Julia said.

"Do you think I don't know that?" Adele snapped. Julia was taken aback to hear harsh words from her gentle partner. Adele's anger was like iron, cold and hard.

They knew Kedzie had arrived at Human Warehouse 44 when she texted them that she had room 214. Dr. Porter Magnim did not send them one word. They reminded themselves that their vow to do no harm extended to him, too. They would not cast a spell to gum up his car, sour his food, or send him face first into a hornets' nest. They pitied his daughter Roxanne, who wanted to be a writer and for whom they had arranged a contact with their publisher. That was the favor he condescended to return.

Kedzie riding with him was a bad omen, a very bad sign. They should not have allowed it. They should not have *arranged* it.

I planted the geranium and the hosta, Kedzie texted. She sent a picture blurred with rain.

We hope you will sleep well tonight, her parents texted back. *Let us know if you need anything.*

Let us know....

I'm fine, Kedzie texted.

Around seven, the witches drifted in. After a bit of chocolate and wine, they drew a circle and settled within it before Julia and Adele's simple altar. North: a stone for Earth; east, a feather for air; west, a bowl for water; south, a candle for fire. An athame, a wand, a cup. An ivory-colored altar cloth embroidered with gold thread. A very old Book of Shadows bound in black leather.

Adele and Julia told the story of the scrying mirror that had shattered when they tried to see Kedzie's future.

"I wonder what you are not supposed to know," Clarissa said.

"All will be well," Farelle said like a child reciting a prayer.

"Was the mirror telling you to keep Kedzie at home?" Toni said. "Or was it telling you to let her go?"

"Maybe the mirror was just an old broken thing," Julia said.

The others, except for Adele, looked shocked.

"I mean it," Julia continued. "Maybe we are deluding ourselves with our rituals and spells and blessed be's. The sacred objects on the altar are just junk; our prayers are self-delusion."

Clarissa, Farelle, Toni, and Menjou shrank away as if Julia had a fatal and communicable disease. Denying the spiritual significance of what had happened to the mirror was blasphemous, possibly dangerous.

Menjou removed from her handbag a collection of curious objects: a pencil stub, a crystal container of salt and another one of sugar, some red paper, and a tiny pair of embroidery scissors. She folded and snipped the paper, then unfolded a red snowflake, intricately patterned. She sprinkled it with sugar and salt, muttering, "sugar for sweet, salt for savor." On the snowflake, she wrote something with the pencil.

No one ever understood Menjou's spells. However, she was famous for doing them. She had some striking Networld testimonials.

"I have done what I could to protect Kedzie," she said to Adele and Julia. "Great forces are gathering. I cannot divert them, but perhaps the blow can be softened. I hope so."

Menjou never used words like "perhaps" and "hope" in connection with her spells. Her unaccustomed waffling frightened Julia and Adele almost as much as the broken mirror had.

"Is she in danger?" Adele asked.

Menjou looked straight at her. "Yes," she said.

That night, Julia and Adele tried to be comforted by the fact that Kedzie thought their spiritual beliefs to be pure fiction. Even as a little girl, she said the prayers and rituals were silly. She used to arrange her toys on the altar. They remembered a doll wearing a mess of colored fabrics, scarves and shawls and little dresses all tangled up together. The doll's arms were raised and her mouth was open. In front of her were little plastic figures, carefully positioned to look as if they were running away.

"Maybe someday," Adele said in the dark of their bedroom, "Kedzie will be the one dressed in a clash of colors with people gathered around her, except these people would not flee."

"She could never have an ordinary life," Julia whispered.

"We've known that for a long time," Adele said. "Ever since that first night when the moon broke through the clouds to shine on her face."

They fell asleep in the early hours believing they'd raised their daughter too well. They did not give her everything she wanted; they actually gave her less in the way of material goods than many parents. But they gave her all the room and support she needed to grow. So her spirit did grow large, and with it her potential. And so Julia and Adele lay there, trying to convince themselves that their gut-wrenching fear and Menjou's warning meant nothing, and that Kedzie would in fact come back to them one day, safe and sound and laughing at her silly mothers.

4

Human Warehouse #44

We have common cause against the night.
—Ray Bradbury, *Something Wicked This Way Comes*

So. We are Comforters at Human Warehouse 44, which was not the place Kedzie Greer thought it would be, not at all. We entered Kedzie's life one by one, in the order you see below, but we speak as a group. We are stronger that way. We have names! Who would have guessed we were as individual as that?

Mona Sadler
Eliza Blue
Gillie James
Juliette Surratte
Pippa Stratton
Alton Feerst
Vane Coniger

We took jobs at HW44 to escape the place where we were born and where we were supposed to die: the UnderWorld hometown of ESY-Backland. Average life expectancy there is about thirty, and a fourth of us die violently. We are supposed to be disposable, dismissible, interchangeable human beings, but we saw what we saw and we understand what we understand.

At HW44 we get room and board, a small salary, and the comfort of knowing that if we shut up and do our jobs, we do not have to go back to ESY-Backland. All of us worked alongside Kedzie, shared meals with her, talked with her, wondered about her, and witnessed how it went down at the end. We tried to warn her. We did.

She did not belong here. To get along at HW44, you need to come from a place where life is short and cruel. In other words, you need to trade up. Kedzie traded down. She descended from a great height to be here. She did some good, but her choices made no sense to us.

Here is how it began: One rainy summer day, Kedzie Greer walked into the dormitory wearing a chestnut-colored jacket and pulling a big suitcase. In one arm she cradled a disintegrating cardboard box full of dirt and green things. Mona saw her first. Mona is the receptionist at the dorm—a plum job. We all envy Mona for not having to work with HW44 patients anymore, in spite of her twelve-hour shifts six days a week.

When Kedzie yawned from fatigue, her jaw cracked loudly. It was the only sound in the lobby. There she stood with her suitcase and that wet box of plants. She had the official HW44 ID. She was supposed to be here, but why?

"Hello," Kedzie said to Mona, pushing the ID across the desk. Mona checked it. Yes, this girl really had signed on as a Comforter.

"You're assigned to room 214," Mona said. What else could she say?

"Thank you," said Kedzie. Whatever planet she came from, she had learned good manners on it.

"Here is the keycard," Mona said. "It opens the room door and the outside door to the building. Everything you need is in the room."

"I brought my own things," Kedzie said.

"I hope you didn't bring too much," Mona said, eyeing that overstuffed suitcase.

"Not too much," Kedzie said. "I'll take the suitcase up to my room. Then I'll come down and put those plants in the garden."

"The garden?" Mona said.

"When I applied for a job here, the Networld site showed garden space for people who lived on-site. I saw the pictures."

Mona stared open-mouthed at Kedzie, trying to gauge the depth of the disaster that was certain for this girl. There are no gardens, of course. We assume Kedzie saw a website put up by HW44 in order to be compliant with some sort of federal regulation. We never did know exactly what she saw. Finally Mona said there was a little group of trees where the plants could go in the ground. Nobody would care. Nobody would notice.

"Can I leave the box here for a few minutes?" Kedzie asked. Mona nodded. Kedzie headed for the elevator, pulling that suitcase full of things she would have no use for in HW44.

In a Comforter's room, everything fits tightly into a space barely able to contain it. Each room contains a miniature fridge, microwave, sink, cupboard, closet, bed, chair, desk, tiny bathroom, and stacking washer-dryer unit. This washer-dryer can handle at most three shirts at a time, or one pair of jeans. A television is on one wall. White plastic blinds hang on the one small window. We get a stripped-down mobile labeled "Property of HW44" for work. We can't roam far in Networld with it, or make or receive calls outside the grounds.

To us, such accommodations are luxurious. To Kedzie Greer, they must have been an eye-opener, to put it very, very mildly.

We liked her, though we don't think she ever quite believed it.

The next time Mona saw Kedzie, she was coming out of the elevator carrying a fork and spoon. She still wore that chestnut-colored jacket, though it was streaked with water.

"These utensils aren't very strong," Kedzie said. "I hope they hold up when I use them to dig holes." She looked a bit crestfallen.

"Just walk around to the back of the dorm," Mona said, because she did not know what else to say. "You'll see the trees; you can't miss them."

Kedzie actually brought the box over to Mona. "One is a geranium and one is a hosta," she said. "The geranium has raggedy leaves and the hosta has smooth ones."

Mona managed two words: "Good luck."

By HW44's little group of trees, Kedzie got down on her knees and dug holes for the plants. The rain had started to fall in torrents. It must have run down and soaked her shoes.

When Kedzie came back inside, she smiled at Mona. "My keycard worked on the outer door, no problem," she said, as if mastering the keycard was a victory. We would find out later about the strange place where she grew up, where people often did not lock their doors and when they did, they used metal keys.

Kedzie's shoes oozed muddy water. She squished her way to the elevator to begin her new life in room 214.

It is easy to imagine her first evening. A hot shower, then lying on her bed in a state of semishock. We at least had been hardened by ESY-Backland. Kedzie had no calloused hide on her. The room fridges are always stocked with mood wine, which is enhanced with drugs to make you feel cheerful or dreamy or sleepy or whatever. However, as far as we knew, Kedzie never touched mood wine, not even when she learned HW44's true nature. She would have had real wine at home. That was the kind of home she came from.

We do know that she showed up for her orientation at 6 A.M. on the dot. She stood there in jeans and a T-shirt, as if trying to fit in with all of us, though the jeans fit nicely and the T-shirt was made of some fine blue-green fabric.

Employees who come late by so much as a minute are made to work a full shift without pay. No excuses, no exceptions. We put up with this rule (and others far worse) because we want to keep our jobs. Kedzie, on the other hand, could have worked every shift without pay with no discomfort. Maybe she was prompt because her parents raised her to be not only well-dressed, but also conscientious. The girl was a puzzle to us.

Kedzie Greer met Eliza Blue that first day because Eliza was assigned to do her orientation. Eliza Blue is six feet tall, sharp-featured and dark-skinned. She looks a fool in the little outfits the girls have to wear: either a blue-striped or pink-striped pinafore over a white dress, white stockings, and white shoes.

Kedzie tried to shake hands, but Eliza left Kedzie's hand hanging in midair. Kedzie did not object, just let her hand fall quietly to her side.

Eliza Blue gave Kedzie a package wrapped in brown paper. Inside were her two uniforms, distinguished only by the color of the pinafores. "They say the uniforms make us look sweet and friendly," Eliza Blue said, glancing ceilingward at something Kedzie could not see.

"What about the boys?" Kedzie asked. Eliza Blue cracked a tiny smile. "They wear pink-striped or blue-striped shirts, white pants, white socks, and white shoes," she said.

"Do they hate that?"

"Yes," Eliza Blue said, thinking Kedzie might be all right after all. But then Kedzie asked her next question.

"Why do we get only two uniforms?"

"They're so pretty you want more?" Eliza Blue said. "You want one with pearls and lace, maybe?"

Kedzie couldn't come up with a response to that.

"Well, go and change," Eliza Blue said, gesturing toward the bathroom labeled with an F for female.

Unlike Eliza Blue, Kedzie looked good in the uniform. The pink pinafore and white dress made a contrast to her black hair and blue eyes. She was a little bit Asian; you could tell from the slight fold over her eyes.

A funny thing about Kedzie: she seemed small but was actually about average height for a girl. The impression of smallness must have come from her seeming younger than sixteen to us. A sixteen-year-old resident of ESY-Backland is either hardened or dead.

Eliza Blue took Kedzie through the easy part of orientation: how to use the HW44 mobile to navigate the building and the grounds, when and where to check in, where to store personal belongings, and the location of the break rooms. Kedzie caught on fast, which pleased Eliza because she hated explaining anything to anyone. She and Kedzie drank coffee for a few minutes. Reunited States coffee is real, by the way. It must not be worthwhile for Food+ manufacturers to create a fake version of coffee.

Eliza Blue stretched out the break as long as she could because the next phase of orientation was Rounds, which is to say Truth Time, which is to say the point at which new hires wonder whether or not they can stand the job. It helps to remember that we would have to return to ESY-Backland if we don't play along. We don't know what helped Kedzie that first day.

Kedzie followed Eliza Blue to her station. She stood quietly and watched while Eliza opened a little drawer and pulled out a bag of Food+ candy bars and a deck of cards with inspirational messages written on them. These she put into the left pocket of her pinafore. From one of the refrigerators, she got a plastic bag labeled ELIZA BLUE. It contained pill boxes and three or four syringes encased in plastic bubble packaging. She noticed that Kedzie went pale at the sight of syringes. "You won't last long if you can't stick 'em," she snapped. Kedzie lowered her head and said softly, "I know there is good in it."

Eliza Blue said later that she wanted to cry for Kedzie that first day. At twenty-one, she was only five years older than Kedzie, but she said she felt like an old woman talking to a child. No one knew she had tender feelings. That she felt sad for Kedzie was absolutely amazing.

Kedzie trailed after Eliza Blue through mazes of corridors. In the first room was an old man sleeping. Like all the rooms, it was the size of a small child's room furnished with a narrow bed, a miniscule nightstand with a single drawer, and a miniature bathroom. There was one chair, no window. The old man could get out of bed and go to the bathroom by taking two short steps.

"Why is there no window?" Kedzie asked.

"Windows in here?" Eliza Blue said. "Honey, if every room had a window, this place would be made of glass." She shook her head and moved toward the door. Kedzie followed reluctantly.

Once back in the corridor, Kedzie asked, "Shouldn't we have done something for him?"

"You never, ever wake them up," Eliza Blue said. "Rule Number One around here is let them sleep."

In the second room was an old woman, also sleeping. That visit did not last even a minute. Trailing after Eliza Blue, Kedzie wondered what Comforters were even hired here for. Of what use were they?

In the third room was a middle-aged woman who was awake. She held a stuffed animal in her arms—an orange kitten with four white feet. "This is Orange," the woman said.

"How is Orange today?" Eliza Blue asked.

"Very well, thank you. Who is that girl with the bright eyes?"

"This is Kedzie Greer," Eliza Blue said. "Kedzie, meet Estie Slake. You will be taking care of her soon."

"Ma'am," Kedzie said politely, as she must have been taught. What world did she come from, where such good manners were apparently considered to be useful?

"I had a cat once," Estie said to Kedzie. "She had a coat deep as midnight and four white feet like this one here," Estie said, pointing to the white feet of the stuffed kitten. Abruptly she began to cry. "Her name was Sadie," she said through her tears. "I had something to love and it loved me back. Me!"

"Sadie is waiting for you on the rainbow bridge," Eliza Blue said. This statement was such a contrast to the hardened person she seemed to be that Kedzie stared at her, astonished. She had known Eliza only an hour or so, but was certain she'd never believe in such a thing as a heaven for cats.

"In all the world," Estie continued, "there was one creature that was pleased with how my life turned out. That was Sadie. I rescued her and took care of her till she died. She was happy with me, glad that I existed."

"Sadie is waiting for you," Eliza Blue repeated. She reached into the right-hand pocket of her pinafore and removed the plastic bag of medications. She pulled out one of the plastic syringe packets, opened it with a single deft motion, gave Estie an injection, put the used syringe back into its plastic casing, and dropped the packet into her pocket. The entire operation took perhaps five seconds. Estie closed her eyes blissfully. "That didn't hurt at all, sweetie. You're good."

"Remember, you can get this anytime you need it," Eliza Blue said.

"I took my Sadie to the vet before her time came, because she was in such pain. When she looked up at me, just before the vet gave her the needle, she seemed bewildered."

The drug quickly took effect, and Estie slipped into a light sleep. On the tiny nightstand by her bed Eliza Blue placed a Food+ chocolate bar.

"Is she dying?" Kedzie asked Eliza Blue in the corridor.

"Of course she is."

"What did you give her?"

"Mojo. Morphine without the side effects—best thing medicine ever invented. It is one sweet drug."

"Do you believe she will see her cat in the next world?"

"Do you?" Eliza Blue asked. She seemed annoyed by the question.

"I was raised to believe yes," Kedzie said solemnly.

"Nice for you," Eliza Blue said. She stopped at a closed door. "This one is going to be tough," she said, more to herself than to Kedzie.

In the fourth room was a young woman bound to the bed with heavy restraints. Her hair was dirty and wild; her bloodshot eyes bulged with panic. Kedzie stopped, as though she had run into a wall.

"Mirbelle," Eliza Blue said to Kedzie as if introducing them. Mirbelle paid no attention.

"I can't lie here," she cried. "I can't lie here, I want to go out." She thrashed from side to side, as much as she could.

"Couldn't we—?" Kedzie began.

"No, we couldn't," Eliza Blue said. She rummaged in the plastic bag of drugs again and brought out one of the little boxes. From the little box she took a little pill. "Hold her mouth open," she said to Kedzie, who obeyed. When Eliza Blue got the pill under Mirbelle's tongue, she shouted "Close it!" Kedzie pressed both hands on Mirbelle's lower jaw, thinking, *This cannot be comfort.*

The pill took effect almost instantly, and the agony on Mirbelle's face receded. Over her exhausted countenance came a look of dumb peace. Her eyes closed.

"They shouldn't tranq her with pills," Eliza Blue said. "She needs Mojo; I've tried to tell them, but Mojo is reserved for people who won't need it for very long, because it is expensive." A brief, bitter smile flickered across Eliza Blue's face.

"She is a young woman," Kedzie said.

"She is mad."

"What is she mad at?" Kedzie asked.

"I mean she is crazy mad, not angry mad," Eliza Blue said, but a shadow crossed her face. "We can't do anything for her. Let's get out of here."

In the fifth room was another old man, asleep. "People sleep a lot here," Kedzie remarked.

"Wouldn't you?" Eliza Blue asked. Irritability flickered in her voice like a fire not quite put out.

In the sixth room an old woman named Paulina wanted to talk about a book about the origin of the universe. "It's all about coils," she cried. "Little coils all different but all part of the One. Everything in the universe has its own coil, every rock, every tree, every snowflake."

Eliza Blue did not respond. Kedzie said that her parents had taught her that everything is part of everything else.

"They were right, except everything is its own self, too," Paulina said. "The TV book explained it all to me."

Paulina's TV was tuned to a newsfeed. It displayed its motto in red and orange:

ALL THE NEWS YOU WANT TO HEAR.

"My parents say that is the motto of all newsfeeds whether they admit it or not," Kedzie said.

"They taught you well," Paulina said. Her eyes shone with pleasure at Kedzie's remark. It seemed as if she might get out of bed, though there was nowhere to go once she did. "I was on a newsfeed once," she said. "Most beautiful girl in my hometown, I was. Look at me now."

"What happened to you?" Kedzie asked, but she was violently shushed by Eliza Blue.

"I tried so hard to be good," Paulina whispered, her face crumpling into sadness. "I pushed my thoughts down, but they wouldn't stay down. I was supposed to be the beautiful girl but if your beauty fades away, what are you supposed to be?"

Kedzie did not know what to say to that. How could she? Eliza Blue shot her a disgusted look.

"For most of our marriage, my husband and I hated each other."

Eliza Blue hastily brought out a pill box with Paulina's name on it. She offered a tiny white pill to Paulina, who accepted it with sudden, massive indifference. "You can listen to as many audiobooks as you want," Eliza Blue said. "You're a lucky woman; we should all be so lucky."

Kedzie trailed behind Eliza Blue out of the room. Eliza felt savage, so she spoke harshly: "Here's why you don't ask what happened to her: She tried to kill her husband and then attempted suicide. Didn't quite succeed either time."

Kedzie recoiled from Eliza Blue's words as if from a blow. Eliza Blue told her not to be so sensitive.

"Are you wondering why she isn't in one of the Hells for criminals?"

Kedzie whispered no, she didn't.

"The woman is UnderWorld. Poor criminals go to a Human Warehouse. Imprisonment in a Hell costs more money than they are worth."

"She seems smart," Kedzie said.

"Except for the fact that nothing she says makes any sense, she is."

"No, some of it does."

At those words Eliza Blue stopped dead. "Look at me," she said.

Kedzie did as she was told.

"Get this and get it good," Eliza Blue said. "As a Comforter, you give comfort. That means just what you saw in those six rooms. You do not have cozy little chats. You do not encourage people to remember the past, which doesn't bring them peace or happiness. If you believe nothing else, believe that."

They took an elevator ride to the top floor and walked the confusion of corridors. Eliza Blue said the design of HW44 was inhuman because workers and patients did not matter. They came finally to the door of room 1212.

"This is a young one," Eliza Blue said. "He's an UnderWorld orphan and he's dying. And he has a lot to say." She sighed and pushed open the door.

Mal had a wrinkled pallor, a gaunt face, a hawk nose, and flyaway black hair. There were large bruises on his forearms from many Mojo injections. He gave the impression of leaning into the wind, even though his room always was quiet. He faced Kedzie and Eliza Blue with the bitter amusement of a teenage boy faced with stupidity almost too great for him to bear.

Mal wouldn't die and he refused euthanasia, though we had to offer it to him every week. When Kedzie met him, he had already exceeded his life expectancy by more than a year. Not cost-efficient, that boy.

Oh, we all remember Mal.

He looked at Kedzie longer than he looked at Eliza Blue. Something like a lightning flash illuminated his features, but it was immediately replaced by the usual mask of contempt.

"Come to comfort the dying boy," he said.

"Come to give you a shot of Mojo," Eliza Blue said briefly.

"No," Mal said, as if Kedzie had asked a question. "I am not dying of cancer. I am dying of something else."

"What?" Kedzie asked.

"Aplastic anemia," Mal said. "I could be fixed by an infusion of biocomputers to replace my sick stem cells, but I'm not worth the price of that technology."

"You'll feel better with Mojo," Eliza Blue said. "No headaches anyway." She jabbed Mal in the arm with a syringe.

"I don't even get transfusions," Mal added with a bitter laugh, but Mojo works fast and got him good and spaced.

"We're done for now," Eliza Blue said to Kedzie. "Follow me."

"How can a half hour of Rounds be orientation to all my duties?" Kedzie asked. Eliza Blue pisses off everyone sooner or later. She is so in your face about her unhappiness.

"There's more," Eliza Blue said. "But I want a break before I show it to you."

In the break room, Eliza Blue poured herself a big cup of coffee and drank it straight down with her eyes closed. Sometimes Eliza shuts out the world by doing that. Kedzie sipped her own cup of coffee, probably wondering what was ahead of her. What she said next, though, was surprising.

"I want to practice giving injections," she said.

"Nothing to those," Eliza Blue said without opening her eyes. She held her face close above the steam rising from the cup of coffee, as if for warmth. "The hypos are sterile, they come in sealed packages—no chance of infection, no air bubbles in the syringe. Just stick 'em and go."

Kedzie said she still wanted to practice.

"Good luck," Eliza Blue said. "I don't know what you'd practice on."

"I saw you put the used syringes back in your pocket. Can I have one?"

"What kind of fool are you?" Eliza Blue snapped. She reached into her right-hand pocket, pulled out the two used syringes, and threw them on the table—all without opening her eyes. Kedzie put them in her own pocket.

"You aren't telling me the truth," Kedzie said. "The shift is eight and a half hours long. You took me on Rounds for what—about a half hour? What do you do for the other eight hours?"

"I do everything. *Everything*."

Kedzie waited for her to say more.

"Change their diapers if they can't walk to the toilet. Feed them if they can't feed themselves. Take them to the exercise room so they can noodle around. Listen to them babble about nothing. Give them tranqs and Mojo. Some of them want to hold your hand, and some want more than that. You decide how far you want to go in that direction. At the end of it all, you watch them die.

"The Rounds are only half your duties. For four hours each day, you work in the kitchens, the laundries, or the trash rooms. I'll show you those places next."

"I came here to work," Kedzie said.

Eliza Blue did open her eyes then. "We have no robots," she said, as one reciting a long-nursed grievance. "Robots are expensive and precious. We are cheap and disposable. That's why we do all the work. We don't even have cleaning bots! Not for us, sweetheart. We aren't worth helping. Come with me and you'll see what we do."

Eliza Blue gave Kedzie a short and instructive tour. In the kitchen, people in blue coveralls darted back and forth. They heated little packages of Food+ meals and opened Food+ beverages and stuck straws in them. Coffee was dispensed into foam cups. The workers prepared trays and put them on great trolleys with twelve shelves, which they pushed out the double doors, down the long corridor, and onto elevators for delivery to the patients.

Those carts are hard to push. They don't have to be so big and heavy.

The laundry room held row after row of enormous washers and dryers. Workers carrying baskets of gowns and linen ran with their burdens here and there among the machines. In, out, in, out—with buzzers constantly sounding. The place was stifling hot and humid, but the conditions had no effect on the pace of the work, which was fast. The floor was slippery with water and detergent.

The trash room contained bins marked for different kinds of disposables: paper, plastic, medical waste, diapers. In this room, too, people worked quickly. Kedzie stared at the workers. She had never labored at grinding, repetitive, soul-crushing tasks. The duties fell heavily on her.

"Is this it, then?" Kedzie asked quietly.

"Unless you want another cup of coffee," Eliza Blue said. It was the friendliest thing she had said that morning.

"I do," Kedzie said. "I'd like to talk."

In a break room, Kedzie and Eliza got big mugs of coffee with a lot of sweetener. Again, Eliza used the mug of coffee to warm herself. It was not cold in HW44; Eliza wanted another kind of warmth.

"I don't know how to do these jobs," Kedzie said, "but I want to learn."

"Why?"

"Because I want to do good," Kedzie said. The simple innocence of this comment caught Eliza Blue by surprise.

"Good doesn't have much room to grow around here," she said.

"I'll give it room," Kedzie said.

"If you don't like it, you can go home," Eliza Blue said. "I couldn't go back to ESY-Backland if I wanted to."

"Why can't you go back?"

"I killed a man," Eliza Blue said. That is a lie she likes to tell. We credit Kedzie for knowing straight off it was a lie. The girl was not stupid. We also credit her for speaking up: "You didn't kill anyone."

Not many things can shut Eliza Blue up when she is riding the unhappiness train, but that did. She felt a sliver of respect for the girl. When she refilled her own coffee cup, she took Kedzie's for a refill, too. However, she thought Kedzie should have known better than to come to HW44 in the first place and this opinion never really changed.

That evening Kedzie got the message that her shift would begin the next morning at six, "not one minute before nor one minute after." She also was informed that the people she had seen during orientation would be her patients. She told us later that this was happy news. At least she would see familiar faces.

She feared giving injections. That first night after orientation she spent alone in her room, practicing with the discarded syringes. To approximate the feeling of flesh, she used a box of Food+ sponge cakes. These are big soft balls of something barely edible, tightly encased in a plastic bag. They are soft as sponges.

It hurts to consider Kedzie trying so hard to do the right thing. She said that she practiced all that evening, until the balls of cake fell apart. She must have wanted to talk to someone that night. However, her experience with Eliza Blue that morning had made her reluctant to be friendly and introduce herself to anyone, to knock on any of the other doors.

At 5:59 the next morning, she was standing where she had been instructed to go: a station on the fifth floor. Exactly at 6:00 A.M., she checked herself in.

It was cruel to put her in the kitchen right away, but that is where she began. She had to strip off her new pinafore, dress, and stockings, put them in a locker, and don a gray T-shirt and tan overalls. She had to sanitize her hands and forearms with dollops of stinging antiseptic. We saw her hard at work opening the numbered packages of Food+ breakfasts, heating them in huge microwave ovens if heat was needed, and setting them on trays. She got numbered beverage containers from refrigerators and stuck straws through the lids. She dispensed coffee into lidded plastic cups and pushed straws through those lids, too. Quickly!—she loaded trays onto the heavy trolley and pushed the trolley into the corridor.

Kedzie had not organized the trays efficiently, so she had to backtrack often, all the while shoving her monster trolley. We were not kind. We smirked when we met her in the corridors and on the elevators, flying up and down, peering at room numbers. You learn to arrange the meals so that you can deliver all of them on a single floor, or two floors at the most. Kedzie had prepared trays almost at random. We were relaxing in the break rooms by the time she finished.

At that point—a good joke on Kedzie—it was time to collect the meal trash and trays and dispose of them. She had to start her back-and-forth and up-and-down all over again. We had time for another break before Rounds started, but she did not. She gobbled an energy bar without looking at anybody.

Her mobile blasted an alarm that split everyone's ears: two minutes until Rounds. She did not know that you could mute the sound of reminders. Everybody grinned as Kedzie fumbled with her HW44 mobile and got the thing to shut up at last.

She left the break room on the run, forgetting that another Comforter was supposed to be with her every day for that first week. The idea was to make sure the she didn't accidentally kill anyone by giving them the wrong injection or the wrong pills, or get patients excited by making the wrong comments. Things like that.

"Wait!" cried Gillie James, who was assigned to keep her company during Rounds on that first day. "Stop!" She had to race to catch Kedzie at the elevator. Gillie said Kedzie was trembling from head to toe.

Kedzie's first patient was dotty old Estie Slake, the woman with the stuffed kitten who grieved for her real cat, Sadie. Gillie had to push Kedzie to give Estie her Mojo injection. That needle terror was real. Shaking, Kedzie slipped the needle into Estie's mottled old flesh. "That didn't hurt at all, dear," Estie said. (She says that to everyone who gives her an injection, including the ones who bruise her.) When Estie wanted to hear the story of Sadie on the rainbow bridge again, Kedzie obliged. "You will see Sadie in the next world," she said.

That was the comfort she gave that first day.

Kedzie had to give five more injections. She told Gillie that she expected one of the patients to die because of her poor technique. She was that terrified. She pushed on to new patient after new patient with Gillie trailing behind. And with every patient, her injection technique was perfectly fine.

Mal was her last patient for the day. He was sitting up in bed watching a scientific documentary on television when Kedzie and Gillie entered. He immediately switched it off and gave Kedzie a searching look. Gillie was not used to seeing such animation in a patient's face.

"Where are you from?" Mal asked Kedzie. Patients rarely take an interest in us, which is understandable.

"Stillwater," she said. "It's an old town by a lake."

Mal lit up even more brightly. He said he knew about Stillwater from one of the documentaries he watches day and night. "Don't witches live there?" he said.

"Witches haven't run Stillwater for almost ninety years," Kedzie said. She looked embarrassed. "A coven named Cerridwen tried to turn it into a tourist attraction for people interested in the occult. They failed."

"Maybe the documentary got that wrong."

"The documentary definitely got that wrong. It's a nice town. Kind of dull."

"Do any witches still live there?"

"Some," Kedzie said carefully.

"Are there good witches and bad ones?" Mal looked amused.

"Yes. All witches pray and cast spells, but not for the same reasons. Good witches take a vow to harm no one. Evil witches enjoy frightening people and trying to hurt them. Witches can be male or female. They are people with jobs and children like anyone."

"You know a lot about them," Mal said.

"We studied the history of Stillwater in school," Kedzie said, but she looked down and away from Mal when she said it. It was then that Gillie knew she was hiding something, but not until much later would we find out what it was.

"What do witches have to say about the afterlife?"

"Good witches believe that when you die, your spirit travels to the Summerlands."

"Does everything end up in the Summerlands? People, cats, dogs, birds, flies? Actually, nix on the flies. No religion worth its market share talks about insects in heaven."

"If all things live in harmony," Kedzie said, "maybe insects just buzz in peace."

Kedzie's HW44 mobile barked a warning: "Fifteen minutes left on your shift. Clean up and get ready to go home."

As if any of us would forget when our shift ends.

"I'll see you tomorrow?" Mal asked. His face was open and eager—a child's face.

"Sure," Kedzie said. When she smiled at Mal, he blinked as if in bright sunlight.

Kedzie and Gillie logged out and took a slow elevator down to the main lobby. When they walked by the door of the executive director of HW44, Banner Boles, he was standing at attention like an overseer inspecting his slaves. Banner Boles was ugly, but it was impossible to pinpoint the source of his ugliness. It was just part of him, like a bad smell.

"Kedzie Greer," he said. "I am the man who hired you."

Kedzie actually said thank you.

"We'll meet again." He dismissed Kedzie with a waggle of his fingers and a slow smile.

Gillie whispered, "Stay away from him."

"Of course," Kedzie said, looking surprised. "He's a toad." Under her politeness, she was no fool. She read our executive director very, very fast, though she did not go far enough. A toad is, after all, an innocent creature—something Banner Boles had never been.

Gillie and Kedzie walked back to the dorm. At the reception desk, Mona told Kedzie there was a Flash Delivery package from Stillwater for her. No Comforter in the entire history of HW44 had ever received a package via Flash Delivery. Mona hoisted a big box wrapped with colorful tape onto her desk.

"It must be food from home," Kedzie said. Mona and Gillie were bewildered. "We get room and board," Mona said. "That's one nice thing about working here."

"Real food, not Food+."

At those words, Gillie froze and Mona sat straight up her chair. Natural food was dangerous; everybody knew that. Kedzie's parents must be crazy.

"What are they trying to do?" Mona asked.

"I've always eaten real food," Kedzie said. "My parents say eating Food+ makes you sick."

"It is okay," Gillie said. "Besides, there isn't anything else."

"All Food+ products contain an appetite suppressant," Kedzie explained, "even the ones for babies and children."

"That's to keep us from getting fat," Gillie said.

"My parents say the appetite suppressant is because eating too much Food+ is dangerous," Kedzie said.

"I've heard natural food costs a fortune," Gillie said.

"My parents grow some of it themselves."

"Wow. And you are still alive."

Kedzie laughed, though she knew Mona had not been joking. She peeled the tape off the package and opened it.

"What are the names of those things in the box?" Mona said nervously.

"Cookies, Indian bread, chocolate cake, and fresh fruit."
"What is Indian bread?" Mona asked.
"It has rye flour and corn meal."
"What are rye flour and corn meal?"
"Just food," Kedzie said. "Have a cookie."

Because Gillie and Mona were not ones to show fear, they each took one cookie from the bag Kedzie held out. They had never tasted butter and brown sugar before; none of us had. They were shocked by the richness. Mona trembled as if she expected to die at any second. However, instead of dying, both she and Gillie felt good. Kedzie said natural food contained no pharmaceuticals, so the sweetness must have been the source of the high they felt.

Experimentally, Mona took another bite. Gillie did the same. "This is good," Mona said in a wondering tone of voice. They ended up eating those cookies straight down. With a smile, Kedzie held out the bag so they could take more. She said those cookies were called Snickerdoodles, whatever that meant, and that her parents had made them for her since childhood.

Kedzie got boxes from home every week and sometimes twice. Eventually, all of us tried bread, cake, and cookies, and none of us got sick or died from eating them. We drew the line at fresh fruit and home-canned vegetables. We did not refuse these gifts because we did not want Kedzie to think we were cowards. We thanked her politely, put the alien food in our pockets, and tossed it in the trasher as soon as we got home.

She said she could not eat all of the treats herself. Maybe that was true. More likely, she was trying to buy our friendship. She never quite fit in, and she knew it. But here is an odd thing: For all her niceness, Kedzie committed acts of disobedience that none of us would dare. We needed to keep our jobs. She could walk away, but we didn't have that choice.

For example, on her second day of full-time work, Kedzie was two minutes late. She ran into her check-in/check-out station just as that loud, crappy HW44 mobile was beeping and yapping because it was 6:02 and her shift had already started.

The check-in station automatically interrogated her: Did she understand she would have to work a day without pay? Yes. Did she understand that if it happened again, she would again have to work a day without pay? Yes. It didn't mean much to her, though it would have been awful for any of the rest of us. We needed our pay.

Kedzie started her unpaid work in laundry room #5. Laundries are hot, steamy places full of noise and motion. You have to pay attention to where you are going. The floor can be slippery, and the carts and baskets are heavy. No one should have to work at high speed in such a place, and outside of human warehouses, no one does. Laundries elsewhere are staffed by cleaning bots.

Kedzie was ordered to put dirty sheets and towels into the maw of one of the washing machines. She did as she was told, added a packet of detergent from the pile on a nearby shelf, and hit the On button. She was directed to remove more sheets and towels out of a huge dryer, and sort and fold them. That sums up our work in the laundry: repetitious and sweaty. Four hours later Kedzie got a 30-minute break. She sat in an orange chair in the break room, drinking coffee, her eyes on the floor. The air-conditioned break room came as a shock after the heat of the laundry. Kedzie was shivering. Her black hair gleamed with perspiration. That was how Juliette Surratte first saw her.

A pretty name like Juliette Surratte may bring to mind a pretty girl. Maybe you think "blonde hair, blue eyes, good figure." That's not even close to the truth. Juliette Surratte is thirty-two years old and has been at HW44 for sixteen years. Her face is pitted with scars. The skin around her eyes is puffy, and her eyelids droop. She wears black glasses we think she picked for their ugliness. Her uniform is never on straight and never quite clean. Her nails are bitten. Her feet are weirdly small. She cringes as she moves about, like an abused animal waiting for its next kick or blow.

That day Juliette had the job of staying with Kedzie when she went on Rounds. Gillie would have done it, but she had been assigned to a night shift. (Our shifts go from night to day to night again without concern about the effects on us, or on the quality of our work.) Juliette's assignment was no more than random scheduling. No one stopped to think, *Juliette Surratte is dull and full of misery, so maybe she is not the best person to watch over a new hire.* No one thought about it at all.

The first thing Kedzie said to Juliette was: "I feel slightly light-headed. I think I'm catching a cold." Then, she began to chatter about the coffee, the weather, and what she hoped to accomplish at HW44. She persisted in this until Juliette couldn't stand it any longer.

"What are you doing here in the first place?" Juliette said.

"I applied," Kedzie said softly. "They hired me."

"Let me ask it again," Juliette said. "What are you doing here?"

Juliette was a stone wall into which Kedzie had run face first. Juliette did not have Eliza Blue's anger. She was a stub of a human being; most of her personhood had been whittled away.

"I want to do good," Kedzie said. She walked out of the break room quickly, as if eager to start her duties. Juliette had to either speed up—she never sped up for any reason—or follow Kedzie as if she were the new hire and Kedzie the boss. She tried to be indifferent to these circumstances, but by the end of the first hour, there was nothing for it: she was for sure annoyed.

Kedzie went from room to room with Juliette following a few steps behind. Before Kedzie left each room, she said, "All shall be well and all shall be well, and all manner of things shall be well." She spoke as if stating a self-evident truth.

"I tell people lies about the good times to come, too," Juliette said. "What a joke on me and on them."

"If you don't believe, your help is worse than nothing. People know when you are lying to them."

"Even in horrible conditions, people will smile at you," Juliette said. She was lost in her dark and lonely place. "I can't take it sometimes."

They went into the room of Estie Slake, who was wide awake and holding the stuffed kitten in her arms. Estie was fretful. She wanted to go to the rainbow bridge and Sadie. Sadie would guide her into the next world.

None of the little comforts worked—neither chocolate nor reading the TV schedule aloud nor *All shall be well.* "No!" said Estie. "No no no." Then Kedzie did something strange.

"I'm going to give you something pretty to think about, Estie," Kedzie said. She inscribed an arc in the air with her right hand. "Here is a magic circle," she said. "In the circle you are safe."

Estie smiled, showing her few remaining teeth.

"Close your eyes and imagine that you are in a beautiful forest. You are in a little clearing that smells of pine and roses."

At those words, Estie frowned. With her eyes still shut, she asked what those things smelled like.

"Never mind," Kedzie said. "Just think of any nice scent."

"Catnip!" said Estie.

"Um, okay," Kedzie said. "In this clearing is one white candle. Light it."

"I don't see any way to light a candle."

"There is a package of matches next to the candle. Use them."

"Oh," said Estie excitedly, "I see them now."

"As you light the candle, think of one thing you want more than anything on Earth."

"To see my Sadie again on the rainbow bridge," she said. She fell suddenly silent. "Oh," Estie said. "Tell me your name."

Several minutes passed, during which Kedzie waited patiently and Juliette gazed at the TV.

"All right," Kedzie said. "When you are ready, leave the clearing and come back to the room. Keep your eyes closed till you are ready to open them."

Estie opened her eyes. "I have seen my guardian angel," she said. "He has long dark hair and such eyes—I've never before felt eyes look on me like that. His name is Aix."

"Aix?"

"He's young and healthy," Estie said, and laughed.

"Do you want your medicine now?" asked Juliette, meaning the tranq with Estie's name on it.

"I want to stay awake and talk more with Aix," Estie said.

"He's in the room?" Kedzie said, glancing about her.

"He said only I can see him," Estie said. "Because he's mine and nobody else's."

"You can stay awake for that," Kedzie said with a smile. Juliette said that Estie was supposed to have the tranq. Kedzie shook her head. It was a disobedient act. She acted as if she were running HW44 all by herself.

"Aix says not to worry," Estie said. "Sadie is watching and waiting for me on the other side."

Once they were back in the corridor, Juliette asked Kedzie what she was doing in there. Kedzie said that she helped Estie imagine a happy place. There was nothing to it. Juliette could do the same thing.

"What was that all-shall-be-well shit?'

"That's a little prayer," Kedzie said.

When Kedzie did the imagination trick for poor old dying Estie Slake, there was something strong in her voice, something to hold onto. It blew away Juliette's mental fog. It was the earliest evidence we had that Kedzie had power not usual among Comforters.

But we are getting ahead of our story.

The next day, Kedzie showed up for work at 6 A.M. exactly, but with a full-blown cold. She was sent home by a supervisor bot. Those bots record the coming and going of all of us. They never looked like they were paying attention to particular workers, but they knew everything about us.

Ill employees are required to stay in their rooms. Our HW44 mobiles have a list of minor illnesses and the days off allotted for each. A cold entitles a Comforter to three days at home, without pay.

At issue is the fear of contagion. There are bugs and there are superbugs, and it can be hard to tell the difference until it is too late. Testing is available, but it is too expensive to be used for every sniffle or upset stomach, especially in a Human Warehouse.

Every Comforter hopes for a little illness now and then, even with the loss of pay. Being home sick feels like you stole something from a store and did not get caught. We envied Kedzie getting taken out of the action right away. She got three days to rest, even though she did feel miserable. She could eat her parents' strange food. She could sleep all she wanted. She could use her personal high-end mobile to talk and text, and game the hours away.

The day Kedzie returned to work, she had to start in the trash rooms. Garbage, garbage, garbage, and all kinds of broken things—everything to be sorted, put in the right bins, or thrown into the fiery mouth of one of twelve black furnaces for incineration. The trash rooms were hot and rank with bad smells. She sorted, lifted, toted, and burned. Again. Again.

After she finished her shift in the trash rooms, she went on Rounds. She saw Mal last, as she had done before. Juliette Surratte went with her, apparently to oversee her but actually in hope that Kedzie would do another visualization or spell or whatever you called it.

Mal was awake and looking sullenly at television. The minute Kedzie and Juliette walked into his room, he snapped the TV off. "Kedzie!" he said. "What happened to you?"

"I had a cold and they gave me time off to get better. I'm fine now. How are you?"

"I am still dying," Mal said. "I'll be visited one night and taken off to the ovens. Out with the old, in with the new."

Juliette gave him a startled look.

"Operation Clean Sweep," Mal said, warming to the idea. "Too many discards pile up in HW44, there is a cost-efficient way to get rid of them."

"I don't believe you," said Kedzie. "That can't happen."

"Why not?" Mal said.

"People would object," she said softly.

"People can't do anything about it," Mal said.

"They can," Kedzie said.

"Ha," he said. "I think I'll take a tranq today."

Kedzie nodded and gave him the medicine. "I am sure you are wrong about the ovens," she said, because in her world such a thing could not happen.

Juliette longed to tell Kedzie that Mal had stumbled on the truth, like stepping on a rusty nail. However, if you want to stay employed at HW44, you do not speak aloud about the sudden disappearance of patients. Comforters were supposed to be composed of neutrality: no gender, no hope, no desire, no disgust, no fear, no pain.

We are monitored all the time. You have figured that out, haven't you? The HW44 mobile does more than send us our duty rosters. It records every word we say. It cannot be turned off. Try and an alarm goes off.

It knows. It reports back.

As Kedzie and Juliette were leaving for the day, they passed by Banner Boles's office. He was standing in the open door. He looked Kedzie up and down.

"Come into my office," Banner Boles said, but he seemed nervous saying it.

Kedzie looked up. "No, thank you," she said.

"Stillwater must be beautiful if it can turn out someone as beautiful as you." God, he sounded pitiful.

"Thank you for hiring me, but no."

"Polite little girl," Banner Boles. "Do you think I hired you because I thought you had something special to offer the human wrecks at HW44? Because of your pure and exemplary upbringing in Stillwater? That town of saps."

Kedzie shook her head as if trying to knock water out of her ears. Obviously she had very little experience with being hated. Banner Boles twisted his expression into an attitude of superiority. Juliette stared open-mouthed at both of them.

We all knew something was wrong with the man, big time, but we kept our heads down and took the insanity without comment. Kedzie, however, seemed freaked out by Banner Boles. To be fair, he got personal with her, which would have given the jitters to anyone.

The very next day, Kedzie committed a major act of disobedience. She commandeered a wheelchair from a corridor where it seemed to have been abandoned. Ten minutes later, she walked out of HW44 pushing Mal in the chair as if it were a normal thing rather than something forbidden under all circumstances. Gillie was coming in as they were going out.

Trying to keep Kedzie out of trouble, she whispered, "There is a rule against patients going outside."

"I know the rule," Kedzie said. She wheeled Mal past Gillie without slowing down. He rode proudly, like a king.

She took him to the little stand of skinny trees where she had put those plants that first day. The trees were not much to look at, being stunted and frayed, but they were nature. They sheltered us; they helped us breathe. Wireless reception was not so good there; HW44 could not always contact us. That was the single best thing about our forest!

Privacy is important, people. Everything will die if it is pestered long enough.

It was in our forest that Kedzie met Pippa Stratton and Alton Feerst for the first time. Pippa and Alton are a couple. (Relationships among workers are not forbidden, just difficult.) You can see them locked in a clinch pretty much anywhere you go. In the break room outside kitchen #5, they are legendary. When Kedzie and Mal saw them, they smiled in a goofy and benevolent way. Of course, they knew of Kedzie by reputation. She was the girl no one had an explanation for.

"What are you doing out here?" Pippa asked. She is a reasonable girl and a straight shooter.

"Mal wanted to be where he could not even see HW44," Kedzie said. From one of the pockets of her pink-striped pinafore she produced a plastic bag, opened it, and took out a large light-tan bar. Alton and Pippa looked on curiously as she broke off a piece and gave it to Mal, who ate it without hesitation.

"This is good," he said.

"It's Scotch tablet," Kedzie said. She offered pieces to Alton and Pippa, who ate them because being in love made them brave.

"Sweet," said Alton.

"Rich," said Pippa. "What is that flavor?"

"Vanilla," said Kedzie.

"It doesn't taste anything like a vanilla energy drink."

"It wouldn't," Kedzie said. "Have another."

Kedzie helped Mal out of the wheelchair and put a pillow against a tree trunk so he could lie back and be comfortable. The four of them consumed all the Scotch tablet. The forest began to work an enchantment. "I wonder where those plants came from," Pippa said, idly pointing to the ones Kedzie had put in the ground with her own fork and spoon. Pippa did not expect an answer, nor did she want one. She liked their mysterious presence.

"The one with the notched leaves is a geranium, the one with smooth, silver-streaked leaves is a hosta," Kedzie said. "My parents gave them to me." She rubbed a geranium leaf between her fingers, releasing a rose scent. She broke off the geranium leaf and gave it to Mal. He took it carefully in his thin hands.

Mal looked at her with shining eyes. His crush was obvious and painful to witness. Pippa and Alton wondered whether she would let Mal do anything about it before he died. Probably not.

"At home in Stillwater," Kedzie said. "I used to row way out on Star Lake, drop anchor, and read for hours. The boat would rock and drift."

Alton and Pippa were floored. Kedzie not only lived by a lake, but she had a boat.

"Are only rich people allowed to live in Stillwater?" Alton asked.

"Some people are rich but not everybody," Kedzie said. "It is what's called a community of consent."

She told what "consent" meant, and Alton and Pippa were floored again. Imagine a village where everyone simply *decided* to live well. Stillwater was a democracy, which Kedzie said was not as wonderful as it sounded. They had tedious public forums where everything under the sun was debated for hours. What really held the village together, she said, was that everyone who lived there wanted to live there. Anyone could sell out and get rich on the proceeds of the sale, but that would mean living somewhere else.

"Why do things have to be so awful here?" Kedzie said. "I mean it. Why?"

No one had an answer for that. We silently munched her Scotch tablet. A bird sang in one of those skinny trees.

"In Stillwater we have disease and death, and stupidity and selfishness and weakness and laziness and every other fault. We have the government's cruelty. People have to earn money. We have to keep our town up and running. But we have a beautiful place where we live in peace and no one is in poverty."

"We aren't like you," Pippa said. "We can't do what we want."

Kedzie wrinkled her forehead. "Why can't you?"

"Our bosses make the rules."

"Why?"

Kedzie could be such a kid sometimes, asking why over and over.

"We can't get the good jobs. We aren't well educated, on purpose."

"You seem smart enough to me."

Kedzie believed in our worth.

"We aren't supposed to be here," Pippa said, meaning the forest. Her gaze drifted to Kedzie's geranium. The four of them stayed in the trees for more than an hour. Messages on the mobiles piled up. Mal fell asleep. Pippa and Alton lay in each other's arms and dreamed of being rich. Kedzie closed her eyes and rested.

"You are breaking the rules."

Everybody looked up and saw a troll peering from behind a tree. He wore a black suit and a black hat trimmed with a black braid. His face was in shadow. Only when he stepped into the clearing did we realize it was Banner Boles.

"It's a nice day, and Mal wanted to get outside," Kedzie said. Her insolence was grounds for instant dismissal, but Banner Boles did not fire her. He reached out, but his hands hung in midair, sad and useless; he was yards from Kedzie. Alton and Pippa felt a chill of fear. Fear was the emotion pretty much everyone felt sooner or later regarding Kedzie's probable fate.

"No pay for you today," he said.

"There is nothing you can do to me," Mal said. He smiled, showing his rotten teeth.

"Wrong," Banner Boles said. "There is plenty I can do to you."

Mal made a weak fist. There was no muscle tone in his arms. His veins were broken from IVs and blood draws and such.

"I see Mal on my own time," Kedzie said.

"You're a fool." Banner Boles turned on his heel and left. His black hat and clothes said, "me dangerous." His face and body said, "me loser." Terrible that such a man had power over us.

The next day he had all the trees chopped down and the broken limbs hauled away. The geranium and hosta were gone, too. On her way to work, Kedzie stopped and stared at the wreckage.

Soon after that, her shifts began to bounce around crazily. Sometimes she had to work double shifts—which meant working seventeen hours straight. She got start times like 7:21 A.M. or 5:46 P.M. She was always coming or going while everyone else was in the middle of their duties. There were bags under her eyes. Her uniforms became as wrinkled and stained as Juliette Surratte's. She could be found leaning against walls for a five-minute rest and sleeping sitting up in the break room.

None of us had ever seen this before, even as punishment.

Here is something we all remember well from that period: little packages of Scotch tablet set outside our doors with a note saying, "I wish we could get together." According to Mona, Kedzie came into the dorm after a double shift stumbling with fatigue. In her room she opened the latest package from home and thought of us. Her eyes must have blurred with exhaustion as she made up those packages. Her legs must have ached as she walked from room to room with the bundles. At five in the morning she did that.

In case you are wondering, Scotch tablet is caramel candy.

We said to her over and over, "Why don't you give it up and go home?"

Kedzie said, "I won't go until my work is finished." No one knew what she meant by that. Our work never changes and never ends. Eliza Blue once found her asleep in the elevator.

One day when Kedzie reported for her shift at 7:46 A.M., she found out that half of her patients had died the night before. "What happened?" she demanded. We told her to forget it. "That many people don't just suddenly drop dead," she said. We said Yes, they do.

On break, Kedzie continued to ask questions. Vane Coniger shut her up with a slap in the face. No one challenged him or defended her. We had no time and no patience for her dangerous babbling.

"Why did those people die?" Kedzie cried. Her cheek was red where Vane had hit her.

"You know what happened," Vane said. "Everybody knows what happened."

You know too, don't you?

HW44 is a kill shelter. About once a month people are murdered in the night to clear space for new arrivals. The oldest go first, then whoever comes up in a random draw. As the truth sank in, Kedzie looked to each of us in turn. She wanted a smile or a shake of the head—something to tell her that Vane was wrong. We gave her stone faces. We would be sent back to ESY-Backland if we spoke aloud of such things. Vane had taken a risk in saying as much as he did.

Leave it Kedzie to miss the point about the importance of silence.

She obviously told her parents everything about HW44, because suddenly her level of disobedience reached an astonishing peak. Her parents sent tiny surveillance cameras. Kedzie attached them to her pinafore, and you never would have known they were there. Even if you accidentally brushed up against one, you'd think it was just a little roughness in the fabric. She and her parents created a special website with live-streamed video from those cameras. The name of her video record was Abuse Diary: Record of a Comforter at HW44. That was certainly specific.

We found out about Abuse Diary after it had been up about a month. (Of course, we had no access to it on our HW44 mobiles.) Gillie walked into the dorm after a shift, and there was Kedzie sitting cross-legged on the lobby floor as if sadness had shot into her suddenly, like a bullet. She was crying her heart out. People gingerly stepped around her.

Gillie got her on her feet and up to her room. There, Kedzie spilled the story. Abuse Diary's viewers thought Kedzie was an idiot who got what she deserved. They said that HW44 provided employment for poor people who were glad to work there. If she didn't like working for a living, she could go back to Stillwater. Anybody who worked at HW44 could leave, but nobody ever does, they said.

(Not true, that last statement. People have left HW44 in spite of having powerful incentives to stay.)

"I wanted to make a difference," Kedzie said as tears rolled down her face. "I wasn't trying to get people to feel sorry for me, especially not me."

"Do the work or someone else will—that is the rule," Gillie said.

"I know you are afraid of being sent back to ESY-Backland," Kedzie said.

"If someone threatened to send you to ESY-Backland, you would be afraid, too."

"I know," Kedzie said, looking at the floor.

"It could be worse," Gillie said, but as she said those words, she felt sad. It was like the ache you feel when you look at the stars. So beautiful, so far away. We chose HW44 and said, "Okay, not bad," because we knew what it was like to live in ESY-Backland. What if life was about more than choosing between abuse and a worse kind of abuse?

Our bosses do not care what we think or want or believe, but when did we stop caring?

We are needed. Even the ones who run HW44 admit that. The patients are less trouble (that is, need less medication, fewer restraints) when someone tells them everything is all right. And it has to be a human; people do not believe it coming from a robot, for robots are no novelty in 2199.

Poor Kedzie and her parents expected outrage, debate, and reform. Had she asked us what the effect of going public would be, we could have told her in a few rude words. Human Warehouse bosses might have been behind some of the sneering comments directed at the Abuse Diary, but maybe not. There is plenty of free-floating hatred out there, and it is safe to hate us.

None of us were there when Banner Boles decided to teach Kedzie who was in charge of HW44. We found out when the lights went on in the night, and an ambulance siren wailed. We ran out to join a crowd gathered around Kedzie lying in the mud, bleeding, her tears joining the raindrops sliding down her face.

5

Banner Boles's Obsession

For the Dwarf as suddenly appeared, waddling along, a fringe of bells on his dirty shirt jingling softly, his toad-shadow tucked under him, his eyes like broken splinters of brown marble now bright-on-the-surface mad, now deeply mournfully forever-lost-and-gone-buried-away mad, looking for something that could not be found.
—Ray Bradbury, *Something Wicked This Way Comes*

Alone at his desk he waited, sometimes into the clear blue hours of dawn. She never came to him. She cared instead for the human wrecks at HW44; he saw her tenderness in dealing with them. But to him she would say not a word, nor even glance his way when he stood in his office doorway, trying to be the kind of man who turned women's heads.

He watched her day and night. Cameras were in every public space: corridors, patient rooms, storerooms, check-in/out stations, break rooms, bathrooms, trash rooms, laundries, kitchens. Workers could even be spied on in their own rooms. Those cameras were rarely activated because workers' lives were boring. However, the ones in Kedzie's room were active twenty-four hours a day.

In his fantasy she visited his office. Her eyes were bright with desire. She was abject and willing to do as he commanded. She showed herself to him. He stayed hidden and protected within himself. He said do this and do that.

What he wanted was her willing compliance. He would hold her in his arms, and she would heal the pain of his existence by the simple fact of her existence.

But first he had to get her attention.

He blew it the first time he tried. Patients were not allowed outside, but she wheeled the young patient Mal out the front door, almost under his nose. This flagrant disregard of the rules gave him an excuse to confront her. For more than an hour he peered from behind a tree at Kedzie, Mal, and two other workers as they rested in a clearing in HW44's pathetic forest.

While on duty, workers were not allowed to be idle except on designated breaks in designated break rooms. But there was Kedzie, leaning back on her elbows, blowing fluff from a dandelion. It was the most intoxicating hour of his life. He thought he might pass out with the emotions that rolled over him. He admired her spirit and wondered what he could do to cause her pain.

He tiptoed out from behind the tree. "Kedzie Greer, you are not supposed to be here," he said. (He wished he had marched out like a man, not tiptoed like a boy.) Everyone looked up, but no one trembled. Mal gave him an unmistakable sneer. The other two workers seemed to be holding back smiles—though to be fair, they were not on duty, so he had no case against them. But Kedzie just kept blowing puffs from that dandelion.

He told Kedzie she would get no salary that day. That was foolish because she did not care. Mal, the dying boy, believed himself immune from punishment. He made a mental note to prove Mal wrong.

That night, as he drank many glasses of mood wine, he considered how to make her pay. If he threatened to fire her, she would simply go home. If he attacked her physically, there would be a stink. An ordinary UnderWorld worker could be raped without consequence, but not her. Furthermore, he had no confidence he could overpower her. She was healthy and fit, and might know self-defense. If he ended up on the floor . . . no, he would not allow himself to think of that. Even if there were no more than one chance in a thousand of his being defeated that way, he could not risk it.

A memory, still raw as a third-degree burn, reminded him of his smallness and weakness. He had never told anyone what happened to him when he was eight. He would never tell. Just thinking of it, his eyes grew red, his jaw clenched in pain, and his hands formed into fists. Despite all his efforts to chase it away, the memory, secure in its dark cave, snacked contentedly on him all night long.

Yet there was a silver lining to that night, as there often was to the recollection of bad experiences. The next day he woke up knowing how to make Kedzie Greer admit defeat. Like all good plans, it was simple. Kedzie herself had given him the key.

He set things in motion with a single order to Jenner Pattee, Manager of Institutional Intelligence at HW44. The laugh was that the plan involved nothing he could be punished for, even though it involved a few technical illegalities. Neither Banner Boles nor Jenner Pattee would be taking any risk at all.

Besides, Jenner Pattee had done worse. So had he.

Then came the waiting time. He made sure Kedzie got double shifts, changes from day to night, and the worst patients. Like a patient hunter he waited in his blind while Kedzie began to tire a bit, to move a little more slowly. He knew she would not quit, because she believed herself equal to every challenge. Someone had taught her to have a high opinion of herself. He was going to teach her something else.

On the day of October 22, he did not go in to work until five o'clock. He dressed himself carefully: a dark suit and red tie, polished black shoes, and black silk socks. He gave himself a close shave and used bay rum to tone his skin. He massaged a good amount of styling gel into his hair, which he wished he had dyed black for this meeting with Kedzie. He worked hard to get his mud-brown hair higher on top and flat on the sides. He must appear to be an impressive man, a man not to be trifled with. When he was done, he looked in the mirror.

He saw an ugly man dressed very expensively. He did not know why nothing he did made any difference. Perhaps that third-degree memory was searing him alive from the inside out.

All right, he told himself. *She might not want me now, but after tonight she will never forget me.* He ordered his car and rode calmly to work. He looked into no more mirrors. Kedzie had a night shift and would work until four in the morning. Then, if fortune favored him, he would be able to make something happen. After making sure the various cameras were showing him everything he needed to see, he settled down to wait.

A little before 7:30, Kedzie walked into HW44. She was visibly tired, which pleased and excited him. Her uniform was wrinkled and limp, and there was a bloodstain at the hem. Better and better.

That night's shift began in a laundry room because he liked watching her sweat. She did not remember to change out of her uniform into a T-shirt and coveralls before she went to work. He ordered a camera to zoom in. She gave the impression of sleepwalking, although the laundry was cacophonous with machine noise. As he watched, she gathered an armload of wet towels out of a washer and heaved them in a dryer. That little white dress and pink pinafore would be a sopping mess by the time she was done.

But it was boring to watch people do laundry, even Kedzie. Banner Boles's attention began to drift. He had videos that dated back to the day she arrived, all neatly categorized. He looked in the subcategory marked SLEEP and picked one labeled "Kedzie has a nightmare." For twenty minutes or so he watched her thrash and cry out. Pretty good even though she stayed covered by a blanket, more or less. That night she was vulnerable and frightened. And so she would be this night, too.

He had hired her the minute he saw the picture attached to her resume. He did not expect her to say yes. When she did, he doubted she would actually show up.

He did not know how to name her specialness, except to say that if she wanted him, he would be saved. Saved from what? His past, his present, his future. Banner Boles was not his real name. He believed all his troubles had begun with his real name:

Porcus Pocus.

What kind of name is that to give to a male child? "Pocus" came from neither side of his family; his parents chose it on purpose to go with "Porcus." He did not understand why they gave him a name with no dignity or pride. He was the sole bearer of their DNA. By his existence, he gave them life beyond the grave. What did that mean to them? *Porcus Pocus.* He did not see them anymore.

He'd changed his name to Banner Boles when he came of age, thinking his life would change with it, but this did not happen. He still was Porcus Pocus, deep down.

As Banner Boles, he acquired some ambition, but as Porcus Pocus he doubted he could achieve anything at all. This paradox resulted in his rise to the position of executive director at Human Warehouse 44. His little joke was that as the man in charge, he made sure the bodies stayed buried. He could laugh at them because the dead did not rise up from their graves. The living did not rise up either, except for Kedzie. Most HW44 workers came from the violent, impoverished UnderWorld community of ESY-Backland. They could be brought into line simply by threatening to send them back there. As for the patients, they did not matter at all.

From the beginning, Kedzie broke the rules at HW44. To punish her, he changed up her schedule constantly: single to double shift, day to night and back again. He made sure her patient list was edited to eliminate the ones she enjoyed talking to, not that this stopped her. (Mal had not been her patient for many months, but she saw him every day.) She cared for the brain-damaged, the hostile, the incontinent, and the bedridden—sometimes ones with all four characteristics. His ambition was to wear her out. He watched her steps become weary, her eyes become ringed with fatigue.

He was betting on a particular quality of her character: defiance. A lesser girl would have quit and gone home to her mother, or in Kedzie's case, two mothers. But she persisted through every obstacle he put in her way.

He called up a recent video he had titled, "Kedzie's back gives out." In it, Kedzie had to change a man who could not rise from his bed. When she tried to lift him, her back spasmed and she fell to the floor. She could not get to her feet except by hanging on to the man's bed.

Another worker named Vane Coniger entered the room to attend to the man, who bellowed without ceasing during the whole procedure. Vane Coniger's response to the situation was correct—there was no case against him. However, Banner Boles was annoyed that other Comforters liked Kedzie and she liked them back. He wanted her to be lonely, like him.

"I won't quit," Kedzie said, though the pain prevented her from standing upright. "They want me to quit, but I won't." That made Banner Boles smile.

Vane Coniger called for a gurney to get Kedzie to the on-duty healthcare worker, who gave her a cursory exam and prescribed a muscle relaxant. She had to stay in bed three days, which was not good—Banner Boles did not want her to rest—but the agony she experienced made it worthwhile. He had seen the tears in her eyes. Well, he had been crying his whole life.

It was going to be a long night. Banner Boles poured a glass of mood wine named Toko. It had a drug to promote energy and optimism. He glanced at live video: Kedzie was still in the laundry room, but was now as wet as if she had dived into a lake. Had she fallen? He backed up the images: she had gone down hard on her behind on the slippery floor. He grinned.

Kedzie's Abuse Diary was supposed to shock the nation. What a laugh. It mainly got comments like, "What did you expect?" and "Leave if you don't like it, stoopid bitch." Both she and her parents had vastly overestimated the amount of compassion Reunited States citizens had for poor, sick people who had never been real to them in the first place.

The Toko wine began to work, and he filled his glass again. By two in the morning he was watching a movie about war crimes with his feet up on his desk. Not until the end of Kedzie's shift would things get interesting. He hoped she would do what she always did. If she failed to follow her pattern, there would be other chances, but he wanted the thing to happen that night. He was ready.

The movie ended just before four. *Kedzie, make it happen,* he thought.

She was gray in the face and wobbled when she walked, but she did the right thing: headed to the twelfth floor and Mal's room. He made two calls, the first to an HW44 employee to whom he was paying a bonus and the second to Jenner Pattee. "Go," he said.

In room 1212, Mal lay on his back with his head lolling to one side. His thin chest rose and fell. "Mal," Kedzie whispered, touching his bruise-mottled arm. He opened his eyes and smiled.

"Kedz," he said. "Fly me away from here."

"I would if I had magical powers," Kedzie said.

"Sit by my side, then, and keep me company."

Kedzie sat on the edge of the bed, but within a minute was lying down. Mal put his arms around her.

"If you believe in the Summerlands, will you go there after you die?" Mal asked. His tone was not sarcastic.

"Sure," Kedzie said, closing her eyes.

"I think," Mal said, "that there is a lot we don't know about death."

"Believe in the most perfect heaven you can think of," she said. Before she slipped into sleep, she felt Mal kiss the back of her neck, very gently.

Banner Boles sat upright as the door to Room 1212 opened. In came a young man with a shaven head and a nose ring. A holstered gun was strapped across his chest. He bent over Kedzie with a rag in his hands and stuffed it into her mouth. He pulled her out of the bed, pinned her arms behind her back, and snapped handcuffs on her wrists. Banner Boles knew from the way her eyes widened that she recognized Jahn, the man at the reception desk that first day who had called her stupid and lost.

Banner Boles imagined terror leaking into her blood, soundless and deadly.

"Kedzie Greer, you are so predicable," Jahn said. He shoved her face first into a corner. Kedzie struggled in vain to break free.

Mal jerked awake. "What's happening?" he said.

Banner Boles laughed at how easily Jahn pushed Mal down when he tried to get up. The video quality was excellent: Banner Boles could see the pain in Mal's face.

Four human-sized stainless steel robots with articulated limbs but no faces pushed a double-decker stainless steel gurney into the room. Jahn twisted Kedzie around so that she was looking directly at Mal in bed, who mouthed the words "I love you."

Incredible, Banner Boles thought. *Absolutely incredible.*

Two robots held Mal down, and a third positioned his left arm so that it was bare and vulnerable. Out of the arm of the fourth one popped a syringe. The robot brought the syringe down in a stabbing motion. Mal's blood spurted. He trembled all over and then went still. One robot opened a panel on the lower level of the gurney. The others hoisted Mal's body off the bed, shoved it inside the gurney, and closed the panel. They wheeled the gurney out of the room and just like that, Mal was gone. The entire operation had taken less than a minute.

Kedzie twisted back and forth like a girl bound to a stake. Jahn laughed and pulled her gag down. Before she could scream, he kissed her, biting her lip hard enough to draw blood. Watching the footage, Banner Boles frowned. Jahn would find his bonus reduced for that stunt.

Jahn retied the gag more tightly than ever and pushed Kedzie out of the room. She stumbled to her knees. Jahn's laughter rang out in the empty corridor. Although Banner Boles enjoyed seeing her fall, he did not like the way Jahn was exceeding his authority. Jahn would end up with no bonus at all if he persisted in enjoying his work so much.

"Are you wondering where the other workers are?" Jahn said in a high, mocking voice. "If so, you are even stupider than I thought." He hoisted Kedzie to her feet and pushed her ahead of him to the elevator. Banner Boles took out a pocket mirror and studied his reflection. In the dim light of the office, he could tell himself that he had polished up nicely. Maybe he wasn't Porcus Pocus after all. Fear and hope made his nerves dance. He got up to pace the room.

Then he heard shuffling sounds on the other side of the door. In seconds, Kedzie would be in his power. His dream was really coming true. Jahn would have to give up his prize now, like a teaser stallion in a stud farm. Jahn was the warm-up act. Banner Boles was the main event.

Jahn pushed Kedzie into the office. Banner Boles ordered him to uncuff and ungag her. The instant she was free of the gag, she bit Jahn with a ferocity that startled both her captors. "Owowow!" Jahn yelled. He sounded comical, like a character in a cartoon. Banner Boles laughed at him.

"Get out," he said to Jahn. "Close the door behind you."

When Jahn did not move, Banner Boles felt a small frisson of fear. He had no worries about the gun; unbeknownst to Jahn, it was loaded with blanks. But Jahn could be even crazier than Banner Boles suspected he was, and might try a physical attack. Fortunately, Jahn only spat on the floor. He tried to walk out like a powerful man, but he didn't know how. Banner Boles made a mental note to reduce his bonus by three-fourths.

Banner Boles gave Kedzie a complicated look. Lust, longing, and pity were mixed up in it. The pity was for himself. He loathed her for the power she had over him—this girl who would run away if she could. The soul that lit up her dark blue eyes enraged him. It brought him to his knees.

"You're pathetic," she said through her cut lip.

"I am," he said, licking his lips. "Come here."

"No."

"You must be hurt," he crooned, aiming for tenderness.

Kedzie did not answer.

"I want you," he said.

"No."

"I run this place."

"I don't care."

"You could meet with an accident and I could send you home a cripple. Or in a coffin. I've arranged nastier things, Kedzie."

"I don't think you want to hurt me."

Kedzie's breaths were coming short and fast. Even in the half-light, perspiration stood out on her forehead.

"I am Porcus Pocus," he screamed suddenly. He clapped a hand over his mouth, as humiliated as if a toad had leapt out. He had not meant to say his true name.

A look came over his eyes that said *love me, poor me*. He lunged for Kedzie, grabbing her shoulders and pressing his mouth onto hers. He wrapped her in a thick embrace. "Take us down," he whispered hoarsely. "Shatter us."

Kedzie elbowed him in the stomach with more strength than she knew she had. He grunted. She broke free. He missed a grab at her right hip. Putting a chair between them, she began to back toward the door.

"Lock up," Porcus Pocus called out with childish glee. A bolt shot into place.

"Let me out," she said, fighting to keep her voice steady. There stood her boss in his expensive suit, trying to be a man. She felt something tremendous rise up inside her. It was lithe, powerful, and invisible to see.

"Unlock that door," she said. Her eyes flashed fire, and Porcus Pocus cringed as if from a burn. Kedzie Greer could save him with her touch. But he knew then she would not. Not tonight, not ever.

"No was the right answer, Kedzie," he said, aiming for pride in the dark. "Yes would have meant you were a slut. In sluts, sluttishness is acceptable and desirable. In you, it is not."

"Let me out."

"Open," he said to the door, which swung back obligingly on its hinges. "Someone will kill you, Kedzie, but it will not be me."

Kedzie backed out of the room. Her steps were measured, slow and silent. Not until she got outside did she begin to tremble with relief and exhilaration. As the rain pelted down, she broke into a run. She ignored the pain in her hip, her knees, her back, and her wrists. She ignored the white van that swung round a corner. She had a notion, fueled by terror and fury, that she could beat it across the street.

She was wrong.

6

Fallow Time

The moon came over the edge of the lake and looked upon Green Town, ... and saw it all and showed it all.
—Ray Bradbury, *Dandelion Wine*

Kedzie remembered tall, blue-robed angels mouthing words she could not understand. It had to have been in the hospital. Before the hospital was a blank.

She had a concussion, a hairline skull fracture, a broken hand, two cracked ribs, and many cuts and bruises. She had been injured at Human Warehouse 44, where she used to work. A van had hit her, but why did the van hit her? Her parents refused to say. Although she had been hospitalized for a week and home at for another week, they continued to tiptoe around the blank that was *before*.

It was November in Stillwater. Star Lake was gray, the mists that crept in were gray, the sky was gray. Silver frost had taken the gardens. Only the houses showed color. The red shutters of the house at 12 Geranium Lane were bright against the drab landscape.

Kedzie's Networld time was limited to ten minutes a day, her text messages limited to seven a day, and no visitor could stay for longer than fifteen minutes. She slept through the day and most of the night. When not asleep, she lay propped on the sofa, not quite all there, disoriented and confused. She was not supposed to think about anything for too long because her brain needed to rest. Fine with her. To Kedzie, the events of October were hidden like rocks in a fog-bound sea.

Anxiety attacked her with panther-like intensity and as much stealth. She might be nibbling a sandwich when suddenly dread would close around her throat, and she could eat no more. At night she was wakened by terror. Sometimes she cried out. At those times, Julia or Adele would hold her tightly. Her parents said, "Remember the good times, Kedzie. Hold on to good memories as hard as you can." But Kedzie could not hold onto any thought very hard or for very long.

She watched the world in wonder, waiting for it to make sense. Neighbors nursed her with good food, prayers, and healing tisanes. On her first walk outside, Stillwater looked beautiful in the slanting light of late afternoon. Her best friend Ella stayed close by her side, ready to help if Kedzie's steps faltered, but the effects of her injuries were fading. Kedzie and Ella returned home to hot chocolate and a pleasant fire.

The pinhead-sized cameras Kedzie attached to her uniform had faithfully relayed every detail of that last night. They showed the murder of Mal, who, unfortunately for human warehouse officials, was neither old nor passive about his fate. They showed the humiliation of Banner Boles.

Julia and Adele followed the Networld comments about Kedzie's Abuse Diary with some consternation. It was pleasant to see their daughter's strength praised, certainly better than seeing her called a stupid bitch, but the praise was nothing more than ignorant idolatry, as if Kedzie had put on a show.

People from around the world sent thousands of messages. Julia and Adele composed a boilerplate reply to all, along the lines of "Our daughter is still ill, but your note is grace to her and to us. Blessed Be." Even the ones who sent hate mail got that response.

In December, they told her what had happened. She and her boss, Banner Boles, had a confrontation. She ran out of his office and into the path of a van. Her parents did not tell her that the day after the accident Banner Boles, aka Porcus Pocus, pointed a video camera at himself and committed suicide. He made a speech before he did it. The first image was of him wearing a tailored suit and sitting in a chair with his legs crossed. Above the chair was a noose, swaying slightly.

"Kedzie, you could have been my savior," he said to the camera. "There is no one who burns as brightly as you." Then he went on to reveal quite a lot about HW44's routine murder of inconvenient residents, which to his mind fell under the umbrella of legalized euthanasia and was therefore entirely justified.

His last words were, "My real name is Porcus Pocus and I deserve this fate." The last view was of him rising from the chair, getting up on top of it with some difficulty, positioning the noose around his neck, and finally kicking the chair away. His neck broke with an audible crack and he swung back and forth.

"I do not think he will find the afterlife pleasant," Adele said to Julia.

"No," Julia said. "Not pleasant at all."

The officials who originally placed Banner Boles in charge of HW44 had difficulties explaining away this event. They had known for a long time that Banner Boles never should have been put in charge of running so much as a microwave oven, much less a human warehouse. He'd been given the assignment only because nothing that had ever happened there had ever mattered. But now HW44 did matter, thanks to Kedzie Greer.

The officials hired a high profile public relations firm, which went into high gear. It broadcast the accident video taken by the van's windshield-mounted camera, thus providing proof that the Intelligence-driven machine was innocent of any malfunction. The murder of Mal was rationalized by claiming loudly and often that he was a friendless orphan who was dying anyway, and after all, euthanasia was legal. Banner Boles was described as mentally unbalanced.

The PR firm directed venom at Stillwater because so many of its residents publicly denounced both what had happened to Kedzie and the conditions in the warehouse. However, they found it harder to beat down Stillwater than they expected. The place was a tough nut to crack. No one knew where to grab it so as to administer a choke hold.

"Would Stillwater take care of those poor unfortunates if HW44 closed?" a female commentator asked. But she made the mistake of addressing her question not to empty air but to the mayor of Stillwater herself. And Mayor Jeannie Rubello, an old woman with pure white hair and startling green eyes, replied: "Gladly. We would run HW44 using the tax money it now receives. We would do a better job than Porcus Pocus, you can be sure of that. However, we do not believe the government will make us an offer."

Kedzie ignored both television and Networld. Her steps and her voice were soft as she padded from room to room in the little blue house. She walked a bit farther every day. One morning in mid-December, she ate a cinnamon scone and drank coffee with cream. Sunshine on new-fallen snow made the world sparkle, so different from fog-bound November. It was not too cold. She went out alone for a walk bundled up in her familiar plaid coat and red mittens. Her steps were steady. Her mind was clear.

Her parents' nearest neighbor, old Animie Johannsen, was out for a walk, too. Kedzie called hello. "So you are well, Kedzie." Animie said.

"I am." Kedzie heard her own voice strong in the quiet air. She kept walking. Where Stone Street ended in a T-intersection, she turned right onto Wellborne Drive, which led to the town square with its library, community center, and little shops. She sat on a bench and listened to her own breathing.

From time to time, someone she knew passed by. Everyone said hello and wished her well. She closed her eyes and let the winter sun warm her back. Her great ambition to leave Stillwater had come to this: a still moment on a bench in its exact center. She was home.

Are you through with flying, Kedzie?

Kedzie opened her eyes. A bit baffled but not really upset, she looked around for her inquisitor. She saw no one.

At sunset, the question still was in her mind. She loved Stillwater and it loved her back. Surely she could soar in a place already aloft. All she had to do was let go and glide. She was not through with flying, no.

The holiday season came to Stillwater as it always did, as a season of light. Her parents sang carols as they worked in the kitchen: *The Holly and the Ivy, In the Bleak Midwinter, Santa Lucia.* Kedzie helped them decorate the little house with pine, holly, and herbs. Then came the Feast of St. Lucia, a party thrown every December 13 by Menjou and Frederick Ankrom, a couple who owned one of the big houses by the lake. Frederick was a software engineer, Menjou professed to be a witch, and they had four children, all of whom cheerfully helped every year with the elaborate preparations. Some neighbors whispered that Menjou cast an obedience spell on the children. Every year Kedzie's parents took her to the Feast of St. Lucia.

At age thirteen Kedzie was chosen to be the Lucy Bride at the feast. She wore the white dress intricately embroidered with red. On her head she balanced the heavy crown ringed with five lit candles. Woven through the crown were sprigs of holly, rosemary, and pine. She smelled the sharp pine fragrance and the burning wax. No electric candles were allowed for the Feast of St. Lucia.

She carried a tray of "light cats"— saffron-flavored buns made by Menjou that afternoon. She and the four little girls who were her attendants waited outside in the falling snow for their cue to enter the darkened house. Finally they saw Menjou standing at the big bay window, beckoning them to the warmth inside. They walked up to the front door. The guests saw them through the window, the little girls carrying single white candles in finger holders and Kedzie wearing her blazing crown. She remembered that the guests gasped and cheered. She walked tall, conscious of the weight of the crown and the risk of burning. In her mind throbbed the words Bride Bride Bride.

A feast was set out on the sideboard, and a blazing fire warmed the room. "Honor the light," Kedzie said, holding out the tray of saffron buns. The house was full of candlelight and mystery. She remembered seeing her reflection in the big bay window: a girl crowned with light. Snow fell on the dark water. A crescent moon hung in the sky. Something very old was walking with her that night. That was how it felt.

That year, Kedzie went to the feast of St. Lucia with her parents as she always had, but she did not feel part of it. At first she hung out by the cookie table, feeling foolish because the other girls at the table were far younger than she. She did not try to hide her yawns when adults dressed as numinous beings recited their parts and the other adults smiled and applauded.

Then the front door opened. In from the cold and snow walked a young girl wearing the red-embroidered white dress, with her crown of candles and her little attendants. Kedzie felt a strong, unexpected emotion: a nostalgic yearning. She wanted to be that girl again, wearing the crown again.

Are you through with flying, Kedzie?

On the short walk home, a mysterious being—it looked like an animated scarf—crossed Kedzie's path. It undulated softly through the night, giving off light. She stopped and followed it with her eyes until it dissolved into the cold air. "Did you see that?" she asked her parents. They shook their heads. Both Adele and Julia had drunk freely of mulled wine. Kedzie was cold sober.

"Stillwater is full of spirits," Adele said idly. "Let it rest, Kedzie." The three of them continued on home without speaking further. Kedzie put on a new flannel nightgown in a black watch plaid and lay down in her cozy bed, thinking of that night when she was thirteen. A crown of candles could burn the wearer to death, yet she had worn it fearlessly. Every Lucy bride did.

December 21 was Kedzie's official birthday because that was the day her parents found her on their porch. She had probably been born around Thanksgiving, but the date could not be pinned down, any more than her biological parents could be identified. They did not want to be located. They might not even be alive. Every birthday she wondered about them.

Her real parents offered presents, treats, and hope for the future. As if from a distance, Kedzie observed their happy, grateful faces. She ate the good dinner they prepared, she blew out the candles on the chocolate cake. They gave her a diamond tennis bracelet that glittered in the firelight.

Except for Ella, all her close friends had left town. Blake was getting training related to his work at Mackay Gardens. He would be back, but would return to a job he liked and a future he looked forward to. Val had gone to the city to take a low-level corporate job. Lucinda was studying ballet in Europe.

Ella and Kedzie visited their married friends Annie and Weland Conklin, who were still living with Weland's parents. There was something new yet somehow old in Annie's face, which Kedzie and Ella were too young to recognize as resignation.

"Stillwater is a great place," Weland said. "I hope to get a job soon."

"Weland just got his Manual Mode driver's license," Annie said. "He can drive without Intelligence now."

"Not many people know how to drive cars," Ella said politely.

"Don't you want a place of your own?" Kedzie asked.

"Would we be better off?" Weland said. Annie was silent.

"I'm glad I'm not them," Kedzie said to Ella as they walked home.

"I don't know," Ella said. "Weland's parents are all right. They have a nice house."

Kedzie tried to imagine living in her parents' house forever and did not at all like the feeling this idea brought on.

Two nights later there was a band concert in the community center. At the end, the band invited audience members up on stage to sing a song—anything they wanted. For a long time, Kedzie had wanted to sing in public—she had a fine voice and she knew it—but before she had been too afraid.

That night she walked right up. She looked out at her parents, who were smiling, and her neighbors, who sat with hands poised to clap for anything she chose to sing.

She chose the song *Someday Soon*. It was old and she loved it because the girl in that song was about to go away with her beloved. She was leaving everything she knew, and the road would not be easy. Maybe it would end badly, but the song strongly implied that it would not. Love would carry the day.

When she finished the song, the whole room applauded loudly. Kedzie looked at her parents. Make that the whole room minus two. The best they could manage were painful smiles. They looked worried and, to Kedzie's young eyes, they looked old.

On the way home, her parents said, "You sing very well" and "We are glad you got up there." They acted no more impressed than if Kedzie had told them about a good price on dried lentils at the grocery. Kedzie felt crushed. She had just bared her soul with that song!

Then came the deep calm of Christmas week. Lights were ablaze on every porch; candles burned in every window. There was rest and feasting and rest again. On the evening of December 31, her parents went to a neighbor's house for dinner. Kedzie was invited, but declined. She wanted to be alone in the house. She had a mission: to look at her long-abandoned Abuse Diary before the old year went out.

There was the video footage of that last night: the murder of Mal, the look in Banner Boles's eyes when he tried to boss her, the change in that look as he realized she was more powerful than he. He turned from Banner Boles into Porcus Pocus in a second.

She saw all these things in her parents' living room in front of a crackling fire. Pine and wood smoke enchanted the air. A cup of cocoa with real whipped cream waited on a low table. Comfort on comfort on comfort. Stillwater defined her, Stillwater protected her. She owed everything to Stillwater.

"But I was there," she said to the living room ceiling. "I did the work, I took the fall." She went to bed before her parents came home. Wide awake, she listened to her parents gently clink glasses of champagne at midnight.

New Year's Day dawned sunny and frigid. Kedzie moped around the house, in thrall to the restlessness that had driven her out of Stillwater the first time. Something was out there, and she was bound to search for it. Maybe she longed to know her birth mother and father. Maybe she felt oppressed by her sweet town. However, she did not know how to make anything happen.

At about two in the afternoon, she got a text from Ella: "U r famous. Look."

Kedzie jumped onto the Networld site in a heartbeat. She saw a young man with a band of colorful, raggedy people, all standing knee-deep in snow outside HW44. The man had reddish-blonde hair and a grin both gentle and laser-like. It said, "I know who you are and what you think. I can see all the way through you."

"My name is Jon Furey and these are some members of my tribe (the raggedy people cheered and waved). We are Øutsiders. An Øutsider is just like you except we are spending New Year's Day standing in the snow in front of Human Warehouse 44 where a girl named Kedzie Greer recorded the Abuse Diary. I suppose you've all heard of the Abuse Diary." His voice was mild and benign.

He said my name?

"Are we in danger?" Jon Furey mused. "The man coming out of HW44 has a gun, but it is loaded with blanks. Private guards never carry loaded guns, even when they think they do. Too much of a security risk."

He smiled gently at the camera.

"Bots, on the other hand, are licensed to kill."

Kedzie flinched. The man with the gun was Jahn, the security guard who had forced her to watch Mal die.

A beautiful young woman took off her red scarf and waved it in front of Jahn like a cape. "Come on," she murmured seductively, whipping the scarf back and forth. Jahn looked confused. For a moment it seemed that he would lower his head and charge. A half-dozen Comforters dressed in pink and blue uniforms came out the door and stopped to see what was going on.

That young woman impressed Kedzie. There she stood, proud and free and shoulder-to-shoulder with the man named Jon Furey. Kedzie could not tell whether or not they were a couple. She did not act like a girlfriend. She had a proud and light bearing;

she looked like someone who laughed easily and often. Kedzie felt a stab of envy. That beautiful woman was far above her, far beyond her.

"There are no gates," Jon said. "Why would anyone want to break into HW44?"

Still that gentle, smiling tone of voice.

Security guards straggled out wearily to do their duty. (Kedzie knew they were paid even less than Comforters and were bussed in and out from ESY-Backland.)

"Get out," one guard said without enthusiasm.

"Not yet," Jon said.

The guard made a sad attempt to strong-arm Jon, who easily broke the hold. In her parents' living room, Kedzie smiled.

"You aren't going to hurt us," he said. "You don't want to do that, even for money."

Jon and the Øutsiders were now standing in the center of a circle of people, all of them paying close attention. Kedzie had no idea what would happen next.

"See, things are really a mess now at HW44," continued Jon. "The workers are grabbing little freedoms for themselves. The middle managers are thinking about suicide."

Glances went round the circle of Comforters. Even on the tiny screen of Kedzie's mobile, it was clear that Jon had spoken the truth.

"Join us," said the young woman with the red scarf. "You'll still be on the margins of society, but you'll have more fun."

"You can't tell without seeing it written down," Jon said, "But the "O" in Øutsiders is crossed out. We cross out what we don't like. Like Sarah said, we have more fun than you."

Her name is Sarah, thought Kedzie. *That's a grownup name.*

"You are going to have to leave now," a guard said.

"Follow us and be free," said Jon. He and his band broke the circle and waded through the snow to their van, leaving bafflement in their wake. The Øutsider with the video camera followed a few paces behind, still recording everything and feeding it live into Networld. No one took her camera away. Jon had his arm around the young woman with the red scarf.

"Who is Jon Furey?" Kedzie whispered to her mobile.

"Leader of the Øutsider movement," the mobile said. It displayed a photo of Jon Furey holding a bunch of grapes up to his mouth. He looked sidelong at the camera, laughing. He wore a black T-shirt that said, Saintly Smartass.

Ella texted Kedzie: "He get 2 U?"

Kedzie's text was one letter: "Y."

Kedzie discovered that Jon Furey was twenty-seven years old, that he was the only son of two computer scientists, and that no matter how many pictures of him she saw, she wanted to see more. The beautiful girl's name was Sarah St. Clair. She looked sophisticated and was probably wise. Many lovers had surely been in and out of her bed. Kedzie hardly had been out of her parents' house for more than four months.

But she was not the same girl who rode away in Dr. Porter Magnim's limousine, either. A boy she cared for had been murdered before her eyes. The man who ordered the death of that boy wanted to have sex with her. She said no, and he killed himself. They both had died because of her.

Kedzie did some research on the Øutsider movement. When she found out that almost no one took it seriously, she had an odd split reaction: anger and relief. She was angry because Øutsiders looked like they had a good time being Øutsiders, and because Jon Furey had gone to HW44 and said her name out loud. She was relieved because if Øutsiders were just a bunch of pitiful crazies, she was off the hook. She would be wise to forget about sending the message she had already composed in her head.

But almost against her will, she spoke to her mobile: "Jon, I saw the video from HW44. Thank you. Kedzie Greer."

She did not have to wait even a minute for his answer: "Kedzie, glad you wrote. We Øutsiders admire you. Jon."

"Thank you for going to HW44," Kedzie wrote. She felt like an idiot.

"You acted heroically. I like heroines."

Kedzie stopped herself from saying thank you a third time.

"You probably don't see yourself as a heroine. People who act bravely rarely think of themselves as being brave."

Kedzie found her voice: "I did not turn back," she wrote.

"That's what a heroine does."

"I like the Øutsider movement," Kedzie wrote, continuing to feel like an idiot.

"You're from Stillwater. You would like what we do."

"What do you mean?"

"Looks like an Øutsider place to me."

"It isn't. It is more than three hundred years old."

"I'd like to see it sometime."

Kedzie trembled. She was glad Jon Furey could not see her.

"When?" she said.

She got no answer. Jon Furey had broken the connection. She sighed, figuring he had priorities that did not involve her in any way. However, several hours later her mobile sang out with a message:

"How about Thursday?"

Thursday was the day after tomorrow.

"OK go," Kedzie wrote. It was an ordinary text message, such as she had sent hundreds of times, except that now the world seemed to turn on it.

"See you then."

With a pounding heart, she retreated to the living room. The comfortable cushions, the fragrant scents, and the warmth of the New Year's Day house whispered, "Rest, rest." Her mother Julia came by with tea.

"You look so well," she said.

"I am well," Kedzie said in a small voice.

On Wednesday, the ache in the mended bones of Kedzie's right hand did not trouble her. She loved the snow on the pine trees. She loved the wreaths on the doors. She loved Star Lake, which had suddenly frozen again that year. She stood with her mittened hands deep in the pockets of her green plaid winter coat, staring at the waves immobilized in the moment of rising, cresting, breaking. So they would stay until the thaw.

She told herself that she might not like Jon Furey. He had a charismatic Networld presence, but maybe offline he was just another loser. These types were so common that there was a word to describe and dismiss them: *Vapes*. It came from the old word "vaporware," meaning something always promised and never delivered.

Maybe she would actually be relieved if he were a Vape.

No, she wouldn't be. That would be horrible. She would burn to ashes if he were a Vape.

She wanted to be Sarah St. Clair, who laughed and swung her red scarf in front of that scum Jahn's face. She wanted to be somebody's girl, maybe even Jon's. Someday soon, as the song went.

She told Ella, who cheered her on the way people do when someone else is having a great adventure. Kedzie wondered, just for a second, why Ella did not want adventures. Then she did not wonder because, right then, she could think only of herself. Anticipation had a hold on her the way winter seized Star Lake and froze it into silence. She waited, biting her knuckle in anxiety.

She had to tell her parents but could not say the words, so she showed them the video Jon Furey made in the snow at HW44. Julia and Adele knew at once how she felt. Kedzie knew they knew, and could not look them in the eye.

"He's coming to Stillwater tomorrow," Kedzie said.

"He must have wanted to meet you," Julia said evenly, "To make that video and single you out."

"Where will he stay, Kedzie?" Adele said. "You should have told us sooner."

"Not here," Kedzie said. "There is a hotel. He can find it."

"We'll welcome him," Julia said, though she did not say it with any enthusiasm.

"He has kind eyes," Adele said.

"Yes," Julia said, "But there's something subversive about him, something dangerous." She began to pace back and forth in front of the fireplace. Kedzie watched nervously. Julia could be harsh when she was upset.

"It is fine just to meet this man," Julia said with sudden, forced cheer. "This Øutsider movement is interesting. I'll look into it tonight."

"Don't," Kedzie said.

"You can't expect us not to be curious."

"I'm just going to meet him. We'll go for a walk or something."

"No worries then," Adele said mildly, but no one spent an easy night in the house at 12 Geranium Lane. With the same forced cheer she had used earlier, Julia said to Adele, "You are right. We have no reason to worry. "

"Something's coming," Adele said. "You know it is."

All the next morning Kedzie leafed through books from her childhood and waited for Jon Furey to text her. When she tired of fairy tales, horse stories, and eco-poetry, she walked into the village square, where she bought a coffee at the little café that occupied a corner of the community center. "Hi, Geena," she said to the girl working behind the counter. When Geena brought the coffee, she shot Kedzie a look a pure envy.

This baffled Kedzie. After all, she had set her whole soul on breaking out of Stillwater and had failed. What was enviable about that?

"How are things, Geena?"

"Good," Geena said, not meeting Kedzie's eyes. "I got this job."

Kedzie nodded approvingly. It seemed like easy enough work.

"Boring," Geena added, "But that's Stillwater for you."

"Stillwater is beautiful."

"Is that why you left Stillwater to work in a human warehouse? Because Stillwater is so beautiful?"

"I'm back now," Kedzie said. She was more bewildered than ever.

"Ah," Geena said. "But are you going to stay?" She turned away to wait on another customer.

At exactly 11:23, Jon Furey messaged that he was on his way. He would check into the hotel by early afternoon. Kedzie wondered irrationally whether he would be bringing Sarah St. Clair with him. Stop it, she told herself. This thing is all in your head, so far.

She checked herself in the mirror. Over and over she fixed her hair. Five times she changed clothes. She settled finally for simplicity: jeans and a deep red sweater she knew she looked good in. Gold hoops in her ears, a plain gold chain around her neck. A little mascara, then too much, then wiping it all off and starting over. She hid in her room, working on her appearance in an increasingly anxious loop, until her mother Julia called upstairs, "Kedzie, for heaven's sake, take a walk or something."

"Let me be," Kedzie called back.

"Better to get some exercise than stare into a mirror doubting yourself," Julia said. When her mother talked in that rudely insightful way, Kedzie became unnerved and obedient. She put on her coat, boots, and mittens, and went out. When she walked by the Bow Hotel, there was Jon Furey, walking toward the door with a battered, camel-colored duffel bag.

He was taller than she had imagined.

She stopped midstride, her right knee bent and her toe touching the ground. Jon Furey turned in her direction. He smiled and half-opened his arms, as though he expected her to run into them. Kedzie did not. She stayed frozen in place, like a deer sensing danger.

He walked toward her, an enigmatic half-smile on his face. There stood Kedzie, with her raven-wing hair and Asian eyes, the girl whom her parents found in a basket on their porch because her birth parents had cast her away.

Jon Furey said, "I hoped we could meet."

She nodded.

"I'll check in."

"I'll wait," Kedzie said.

They walked together into the vast lobby of the Bow Hotel, lined with floral sofas and overstuffed chairs. The place, Kedzie knew, was largely unoccupied in the winter. It took Jon Furey only a minute to get his room key, an ornate thing such as had not been used in more than a hundred years outside of Stillwater. Inside Stillwater, most everyone used keys like that.

He went up to his room. Kedzie sat down on one of the flowered sofas. He was back before she was ready to see him again.

This time he gave her a real smile. "Show me where you live," he said. It seemed he wanted to cover every square foot of Stillwater. Kedzie had noticed this before among visitors. They wanted to examine all the nooks and crannies because they could not believe the place was real. That ordinary reaction reassured her somewhat. Maybe Jon Furey was not so remarkable after all. Kedzie's cheeks were pink with the cold. She led Jon Furey through Stone Street, Wellborne Street, Angelique Street, Revere Street, Dulci Road, and finally down Water Street to Star Lake with its waves frozen in midcrash like an ice sculptor's fantasy.

"Was that your school?" Jon asked, pointing back at the large brick building on the corner of Water and Revere streets.

"That's Stillwater Omni," Kedzie said. "Yes."

"How did the town get its name?"

"The town was founded by Garvis Stillwater in 1870. His descendent Cassie Stillwater lives in that house over there." Kedzie pointed to a sand-colored house on Water Street. Smoke drifted out of its chimney. Birds twittered around a feeder.

"You know that in 2199 no one attends school in an actual building."

"I know. I didn't mind."

"What a place," Jon said, shaking his head in disbelief. "It can't be real."

"Stillwater isn't backward," Kedzie said.

"No, it's not. I'd call it highly advanced."

They left the lakeshore and walked into the town square. Kedzie watched Jon's surprise at the bounty of goods and services. There was the grocery, the drug store, and the ancient gray-stone library. The library earned another hard look from Jon; Kedzie suspected he had never seen one. There was a primary care medical group, a dentist, a small restaurant called Hearty's, and an art gallery/museum. The largest building was the community center, which was Stillwater's town hall, coffeehouse, and nightclub of sorts.

She and Jon bought mugs of coffee from her ex-schoolmate Geena. Kedzie could feel Geena watching them as they walked to a table and stripped off their coats, scarves, hats, and gloves. She wondered if Geena knew anything about the Øutsider movement. Not likely.

"Are you all right now?" Jon asked.

"I'm all better," Kedzie said.

"You did a great thing working in Human Warehouse 44."

"Great? I don't think so. The other Comforters work just as hard and long, and they can't get away except to go back to a place way worse than Human Warehouse 44."

"You got me there," Jon said. "Then you got me here."

Kedzie shied away from the emotion that overwhelmed her. She sipped her coffee.

"What did Garvis Stillwater do before he built your town?"

"He was in business and very wealthy. He decided he had enough money."

Jon smiled as if Kedzie had said something profound. "You can turn your life around in five minutes if you have the courage," he said. "Five minutes is about all it takes, too."

"Stillwater wasn't built in five minutes."

"It sounds like Garvis Stillwater made the decision in less time than that."

"He wrote that he did," Kedzie said. "We had to read his autobiography in school."

She fiddled with her coffee mug, turning it round and round. Was this real? The coffee mug was firm and smooth in her hands. Yes, this was really happening.

"I'd like to see your house and meet your family," Jon said.

Kedzie cringed. Inside the town's boundaries, no one thought there was anything strange about two lesbians/witches/best-selling authors raising a baby they found in a basket on Yule Eve. However, in the greater scheme of things, it was fairly unusual.

"All right," she said. She messaged her parents but got no answer. She hoped they would not be spell casting when she and Jon walked in, or reading the Tarot.

They were reading the Tarot using their old Ryder deck. Kedzie recognized a spread called a Tetrakyts. Jon's gaze fell on a statuette of a woman dressed in black robes, holding a crystal ball in her bony fingers. However, he did not act repulsed by any of these things. Perhaps he wrote her parents off as one more quaint element in this quaint town.

"You do not lead conventional lives," Jon said. His sweeping glance took in the entire living room, including the several bookcases filled with strange old books such as *Hidden Tarot, The Fairy Faith in Celtic Countries*, and the *Book of Shadows*. A tiny crescent moon on a dark blue base gleamed in the gentle light from a beeswax candle.

"It looks like an easy life, but it is not," Adele said. "Exhausting every hour, to reach for the stars. We sleep well at night, though."

"I've been reading about the Ødutsider movement," Julia said to Jon. "Isn't it sort of silly?"

Kedzie shot her mother a look full of daggers.

"You mean because we disrupt things?" Jon said, not seeming at all offended.

"Do people change because you make humorous observations?"

"We tell truthful jokes," Jon said. "People laugh, then think about what they are laughing at. Some join us."

"What do you gain from all this?"

"We have fun," Jon said with a smile.

Julia arched her eyebrows, but said nothing.

"I've never met real witches," Jon said.

"We won't cast a spell on you," Julia said.

"Though we could," Adele added.

Kedzie sat back in exasperation. She had heard and seen her parents' spells. Often she had to participate in them. They were nothing more than role-playing games. *You enter a clearing in an old-growth forest where you see a tall blonde woman in a green dress who wears a gold medallion. She must answer honestly a question honestly posed, so you ask whether she is good or evil. If she says she is good, you ask her to give you the medallion....*

"Don't threaten Jon with one of your spells," Kedzie said.

"We didn't," Julia said serenely.

Kedzie was baffled by the fact that Jon was not irritated by any of this. On the contrary, he seemed to enjoy talking with her parents. He said to them what he had said to her: five minutes of courage at the right time could smash an old reality to pieces. He gave the example of what he and his followers had done at Human Warehouse 44. "Because of the video of that event, Kedzie contacted me. Because she contacted me, I contacted her. And here we are, the four of us together."

"And what is the significance of the four of us sitting together?" Julia asked.

"You know what it is," Jon said pleasantly.

After an excruciating conversational caesura, Kedzie suggested that she and Jon have dinner at Hearty's. She knew only one thing on earth: she could not sit any longer in the same room with both Jon and her parents.

From the window, Julia and Adele watched them walk toward the town center, not touching. Children think they are clever at hiding the truth from their parents, but Julia and Adele had always found Kedzie transparent, never more than now, when she was trying to hide how she felt about Jon Furey.

At Hearty's, a fire crackled in the fireplace, the food was simple and natural, and it was quiet enough to talk, without any pressure to speak.

"Your parents are nice witches," Jon remarked. "I want to read their books."

"The books aren't very witchy."

They spoke only about the cold night as they walked back from the restaurant. Outside the Bow Hotel, Jon took Kedzie in his arms and kissed her. Kedzie wanted him; her whole soul ached with wanting him. He was excited; he was flattered; he was hopeful about the night.

When she got home, Kedzie drank a cup of mulled wine with her parents by firelight and went up to bed as if she meant to stay there. She thought she had fooled her parents about her intentions. Undeceived, Julia and Adele watched her climb the stairs.

They could sit in the living room until Kedzie came creeping down the stairs to put on her coat and sneak out to meet Jon Furey at the Bow Hotel. At that point they could force her into having a reasonable discussion. Then Kedzie could either storm out the door or briefly bide her time. She was legally an adult. As the law prescribed, she had been eligible for free access to birth control since the age of fifteen. Although she had this right, her parents were sure she had never used it.

Being reasonable would not work. At best, it would delay the inevitable by days or perhaps only by hours. As moonlight poured through the diamond-paned windows, they went arm in arm upstairs to bed.

They had always been frank about sexual attraction. Sex was not the mystery. What happened afterward was the mystery. Kedzie might become smitten with Jon Furey, whose feelings Julia and Adele could not read. They did not trust him.

Around midnight they heard Kedzie slip out of her bedroom and quietly, so very quietly, go downstairs. She put on her green plaid coat and a black beret. Her hands were warm inside double-up mittens: a white pair inside a red pair. She walked through the silent, snowy streets of Stillwater to the Bow Hotel. Lights twinkled on porches; wreaths hung on doors. Ivory moonlight touched the houses and quiet walkways. The moonlight cut a wide swath across the surface of Star Lake and made it shimmer.

As she strode toward the hotel, her bootprints deep and firm in the snow, she remembered how she felt at thirteen as the Lucy Bride among the guests at the Feast of St. Lucia. A crown of candles burned on her head, and her red-trimmed white gown swept the floor. She trembled, but did not stop walking.

A nursery rhyme came back to her: "I see the moon / And the moon sees me / God bless the moon / And God bless me."

Because she knew everybody in Stillwater, she knew the desk clerk on night duty at the Bow Hotel. (Why did the place even have desk clerks? They were unnecessary at every other hotel in the Reunited States.) He looked at her quizzically. Kedzie forced a smile and walked on past his desk.

In front of Jon Furey's door she hesitated for the first time. He wanted her to be here, didn't he? She wasn't wrong about that, was she? Three quiet taps and it would be done.

She knocked on the door. Jon Furey opened it.

"Come in," he said, as if he'd been expecting her all along. That lightning smile! Those kind eyes! Kedzie wavered on the doorstep, unable to move. When she walked through that door, everything would change. Jon reached out and took her hand. He led her in like a child.

There they stood with so little space between them. Conversation went off a cliff. Kedzie had never experienced this sort of closeness.

She threw herself headlong at Jon, not caring that she didn't know what she was doing or that he might laugh. It was like diving into Star Lake and swimming, swimming, swimming with the rough water all around. When Jon kissed her, her body began to sing. That night the Lucy Bride with her burning crown took her place among the grownups.

The next morning at Hearty's, Kedzie and Jon ate bacon and eggs and toast with apricot jam and drank big mugs of coffee. Kedzie's soul surged with the question: Can I go away with you? Yes would open a door. No would close it. She did not have nerve enough to speak. Too much, too soon—but this could not be the end of them, in this little restaurant.

It was snowing lightly when they left. "Let's walk by the water," Kedzie said. With its wild, frozen waves, Star Lake looked like a portal to some other world.

"I've never seen any place like Stillwater," Jon said.

"I don't want to stay here," Kedzie said. *There!* she thought. *Now he must say something in return.*

"You don't have to," Jon said, a little too mildly to suit Kedzie's frame of mind.

"I know I don't have to," she said, not mildly at all.

"I started the Øutsider movement to tell the truth," Jon said, as if to himself. He began to walk faster. Kedzie had to break into a half-run to catch up to him. They were all the way back to the Bow Hotel when he stopped, turned, and caught Kedzie by the shoulders.

"Join us," he said. "Come away with me."

Kedzie looked up at him. Had she heard right? Jon turned on that laser smile of his. He nodded. She threw her arms around his neck like a child.

When Kedzie walked through the door of her parents' house, Julia and Adele sensed a change in her. Of course they knew

Kedzie had stayed out all night, and why, but it was more than that. They perceived no trace of the gentle and quiet convalescent who had been content to stay in Stillwater, if not forever, for a good long time. Their bound-for-glory daughter was back.

Kedzie looked first at Julia, then Adele. Such a calm, steady gaze it was. "I'm going away with Jon Furey tonight," she said.

Julia and Adele had no way to tell their daughter that she was acting like a teenager in love, at least no way she would acknowledge as possibly true. They could rant and rave, but in the end their anger would push Kedzie farther away. She would leave in a rage. They would cry all night.

Kedzie was of age; they could do nothing to prevent her leaving. Taking the job at Human Warehouse 44 had nearly killed her. But working at HW44 was a weak cup of tea compared with the adventure awaiting their daughter, who was giving up everything to run away with a man she barely knew.

7

All for Love

Some folks' polarities are negative, some positive. Some glow in the dark. Some snuff out. You now, the two of you...
—Ray Bradbury, *Something Wicked This Way Comes*

My name is Matreca Benederet Talmadge, and I never should have been born. Most girls with my condition die in the womb, one way or another. But here I am.

My condition has a name but my parents never spoke it. Instead they said, "Never doubt that you are beautiful." They said, "Reach out and take what you want." They said these things through years of pills, shots, specialists, surgeries, scans, and mostly bad prognoses.

I've got funny-looking kidneys. Ask me if I care. I am the daughter of two tall dancers, but needed growth hormones to get to almost five feet tall. That one still bothers me a little.

I know who Kedzie Greer is, of course, but never paid her much mind until I heard her sing one night at a concert in the community center. This was after she got hurt at Human Warehouse 44 and came home, but before she ran away with Jon Furey. Our town has a lot of musicians, so the concert was better than you'd think. At the end, anybody could get up to sing with the band. Kedzie did, and my God, the girl did surprise everyone. She chose a song called *Someday Soon*. The band had never heard of it, but followed her well enough; as I said, this town has more than its share of talented people. She hit the notes just right and gave the words meaning.

However, *Someday Soon* gave me a creepy feeling. The girl in the song was going away with some cowboy, and she didn't sound up to it. By that I mean, her whole way of being with him was to do everything his way—give and give like he was a god and she just a poor helpless girl. That was not the kind of relationship my parents had, or the kind I have with my husband. It simply is not a winning hand.

Kedzie sang about not being afraid to follow this man down a tough road. Except for her brief time at HW44, what tough roads has she known? Her whole life has been spent in this enchanted town: loved and cherished by her parents, blessed with intelligence, beauty, health—this surely has been an easy path. She had a fine singing voice though, and sounded like she meant every word. Everybody in the community center sat straight up and paid attention while she sang the song about a good, innocent girl wanting to live her life the hard way.

What she did as part of the Øutsider movement, on stage and in Networld, was a bigger version of her singing in the community center. She has the power to draw good people into her orbit and to make evil people hate her. Those powers were a problem from our puppet governors' point of view.

She said, "You can set the world on fire." Meaning, I suppose, that if you live passionately you astound pretty much everyone. My mama and papa set the world on fire when they danced. I saw that. They taught me not by talking but by living. I don't hold much with speeches.

I live in Stillwater with my husband Lennon Jones and our five-year-old daughter Cerrie. Cerrie's full name is Cerelia Janette Jones. Janette was my mama's name. You pronounce it "JAHN-ette." She was Irish and West Indian. My papa's name was Marc. He was Greek and English.

Lennon says Cerelia is a Latin word meaning "of the spring." He can speak, read, and write ten languages, Latin being one of them. That is what brought us together. One night, backstage after one of my mama and papa's dance concerts, a girl who didn't speak English tried to convey something to my mama, flapping her hands and struggling with words. Standing nearby was my future husband, and he translated back and forth between the girl and my mama, nice as you please. I did notice him for that.

Forgive me. My mind jumps around. I can't help it, so you will have to jump with me. It is nothing to be ashamed of. Lennon loves the way I talk.

I saw Kedzie and her lover Jon Furey together the last day she was ever in Stillwater as her parents' child. Although it was February and well below zero outside, our apartment was warm as toast. My little girl Cerrie was sitting on the floor working a puzzle with great concentration.

I peered over her shoulder, trying to perceive what she saw so easily. I have never been able to figure how one shape fits into another. When I buy frozen food, I have to ask my husband Lennon to put the items away in a good, orderly arrangement because I cannot do it myself.

Cerrie tried to teach me what I will never be able to learn. That day she patted my hand and said, "Don't worry, Mama. I will show you how." She handed me a puzzle piece and asked me to show her where it went. I turned it this way and that, and hesitatingly tried to make it fit somewhere it wouldn't go.

"But you came close, Mama!" Cerrie said. "We'll get this puzzle solved someday."

My beloved Cerrie makes the world bright.

To hide the tears in my eyes, I pushed myself to my feet and looked out the window. There were Kedzie and Jon Furey outside on this below-zero day. She was all bundled up in a green coat, black beret, and red mittens. He wore a heavy jacket that might have been gray or might have been olive drab.

Something about the way their bodies inclined toward each other made tears come to my eyes all over again. It was like being at a wedding. Kedzie looked up at him with an expression I could understand from across the street. She turned around and waved at her mamas on the porch of the house on Geranium Lane. Then she got into Jon Furey's car and was gone.

Jon Furey led the Øutsider movement, but let me tell you, she was the one who made it catch fire. That girl burned herself up like a rocket heading for the stars. Jon Furey was like a man who got his tie caught in the rocket before it blasted off and had to fly along beside it, wishing he had worn something different.

Lennon and I looked at early videos of Jon Furey and the Øutsiders, made before Kedzie joined up. We couldn't see why anyone would get all that excited. Jon Furey spoke in such a mild way. Lennon said he had a wicked sense of irony, which he explained meant that Jon Furey saw the contradictions between how things appeared and how they really were. There is a powerful lot of irony in the Reunited States in 2199.

Jon Furey struck me as something of a lightweight, though very bright. Lennon felt the same. While Kedzie spoke, Jon Furey stood in the background. That last day in Stillwater when Kedzie looked up at him like a bride taking vows, I could not see his face.

The definition of an Øutsider is simple: someone who has a secret life. No matter what they do, a part of them lives in the shadows. Øutsiders can be poor or prosperous, old or young, men or women. What they have in common is this: a self nobody knows. They stay hidden from everyone except each other. They have codes and signs and secret questions to tell whether you are one of them. But if you don't know the signs and signals, they are invisible.

Life is hard, and it is worse if you are somebody's slave no matter how big a salary you make. If you slave for someone, you have a secret life.

After Kedzie joined the Øutsider movement, it became popular on a scale I doubt Jon Furey ever dreamed of. People chose to hire Øutsiders and work for Øutsiders, and trade at Øutsider businesses. People learned the signs and signals.

Five months ago, a multinational bank named InterGold suddenly turned Øutsider. Tens of thousands of people around the world and billions of dollars were affected. InterGold used the standard channels to check the professional skills of job applicants, but they also asked strange questions such as, "What do you like to do?" and "What are your saddest and happiest childhood memories?" or "How would you describe a perfect day?" Believe me when I say that InterGold's hires worked hard to keep their jobs.

It was the turning of the bank, I think, that made our puppet governors decide to act.

At first the puppets turned up the heat under their fracking operations. Fracking is an advanced form of bullying. It has been around as long as Networld has. Its purpose is the destruction of a human being without breaking the skin.

We in Stillwater are getting fracked without discrimination. Kedzie's parents gave the frackers plenty to work with, being published authors, professed witches, and married lesbians, but almost everybody got hit.

Here's a funny thing: although Kedzie was adopted, the frackers never said a word about her biological family. That impressed the heck out of everyone in Stillwater. It meant that even the government could not trace Kedzie's origins.

Lennon was mocked for his choice of wife—that is to say, me. I was mocked for having been born imperfect. They did not bother with Cerrie, except to say *Poor girl, having a defective mother.* It's true that healthcare workers acted as if my pregnancy was practically an immaculate conception. They didn't think I could ever do anything normally.

Imagine the life of a fracker: Get up, eat breakfast, stab people where it doesn't show. (I don't mean Lennon and me. We are immune.) I wonder how they talk to each other, or if they mention their work at all. Frackers are not paid to have opinions about what they do.

The head fracker of Stillwater was a government employee named Po Moss. We were not supposed to know that, but Øutsiders have spies everywhere now and naturally they tell us things. He was the one who called Kedzie's parents "devil worshippers." He posted fake videos of them being raped, and having sex with animals and demons.

Po Moss sneered at Stillwater for its tiresome democracy in which everyone has a voice, its insistence on civility, and its enclosing gates, which he called "hypocrisy times ten thousand." He operated under a number of aliases, all known to us, thanks to the spies. Using the name "Wild Child," he encouraged people to gather outside the gates and demand to be let in. "They won't permit that. Stillwater permits nothing it fears and dislikes, such as the truth."

When no mob manifested outside our gates (which, by the way, are much less friendly than they used to be), Po Moss arranged to pay cash money to anyone who would join his protest. He managed to gather some hungry "volunteers" who stood outside the gates on a foggy day in the rain, firing old shotguns into the air and chanting, rather dispiritedly, "Let us in." Lennon walked out to take a look and reported what pitiful specimens they were. Even for money, maybe *especially* just for money, these people couldn't do more than go through the motions.

Howie Rubello, the mayor of Stillwater, ordered the gates opened. In came the dripping, bewildered herd. We appeared out of the fog by twos and threes and fours to surround them. It is a myth that everyone in Stillwater is unarmed. We mostly keep our guns in fingerprint-protected safes, but we brought them out for this special occasion.

I could not go out because of Cerrie. However, Lennon stood on the front line, gun in hand, toe to toe with Po Moss's raggedy bunch. I shivered with pride to see him so. The paid mob lost interest and dribbled back toward the gates. I think we could have turned them away with no weapons at all.

Po Moss claimed that Stillwater residents who owned weapons were hypocrites. At that point, he must have been sweating in desperation. We learned he was fired before the day was out. I wonder what he is doing now.

Right after Po Moss failed to harm Stillwater, Kedzie and Jon came to Stillwater. Kedzie made a speech. She wore black trousers and some kind of deep-cut red and purple blouse. Lennon, Cerrie, and I went. Pretty much the entire town was there. The early arrivers crowded into the community center, and the rest spilled out in every direction into the town square. Kedzie smiled upon us as if she was glad to be home. She jumped down to hug her best friend Ella, who had gotten engaged to a boy named Blake Braden. Then she climbed back on stage and directed her attention toward the videocam.

"People of Stillwater," she said, "nothing said about me, my parents, or my town is true. You know lies; you have heard them your entire lives. You can shut them down with a single choice. Walk away as we are walking away now."

We clapped and cheered for this strange girl who seemed to have the world by the tail. I do not think she and Jon Furey were pleased with each other that night. Maybe he didn't want to be there. Maybe the Øutsider movement had gotten too dangerous. Only three days later they were arrested.

Our puppet governors took down Kedzie and Jon oh so very publicly. An entire regiment of Enforcers with guns arrested them at a big outdoor meeting. There was much noise, and water cannons and tear gas, and people screaming and scattering in the chaos. The Enforcers threw Kedzie into the back of a van. They threw Jon into a pond and watched him nearly drown. It's all over Networld.

Here is a thing I remember: Jon Furey looked unhappy from the first minute he stepped on that stage, which was a good half hour before the Enforcers showed up. He did not raise his eyes or give Kedzie a smile. She talked about freedom; a band played some sweet jazz. He might as well not have been there at all.

The puppets charged Kedzie with something so bizarre I can barely write it down: practicing witchcraft for the purpose of sedition. Sedition is a brand new crime and one which is retroactive. That means you can be accused of sedition for something you did before there was any such thing. It means whatever the puppets want it to mean. I don't remember how they defined sedition for Jon Furey. Probably his crime was just telling the truth, which he did long before Kedzie arrived without anyone taking particular interest because he did it with humor and a smile.

The way I figure the witchcraft charge is that the puppets can't explain Kedzie's power over people any other way. That plus the obvious reason: Kedzie's parents profess to be actual witches. The puppets accused her of ridiculous things such as casting spells to boost the Øutsiders' popularity and sticking pins in little dolls to bring grief to her enemies. They imprisoned her for these things she never did, for being a creature that she is not and never has been, a creature that does not even *exist*.

I do not think the e-beasts were behind the arrests. Why would they care about the Øutsider movement? The Dreadful Night want a pure and pristine Networld for themselves. If they care about anything else, no one knows what it is. They don't have a clue about the reality of human life or life on Earth generally.

The Dreadfuls made it clear they were in charge, but not what they wanted to do or wanted *us* to do. They mainly imposed fees for Networld use and enforced harsh standards for companies that operate in Networld, meaning all of them.

Sometimes they punish people who commit crimes. Other times they don't. A year ago they instituted a Play Day, on which government employees got a paid day off. While they were relaxing, the Dreadfuls randomly compromised thousands of bank and credit accounts. Our leaders do love to laugh.

Here is one thing I am sure of: the Dreadful Night are not the only e-beasts in Networld. I think there are a zillion e-beasts out there, just as there are all kinds of people. The Dreadfuls got power because they wanted power, and the other e-beasts had more sense than to want it. The Dreadful Night must be a swarm of idiotic e-beasts indeed, wanting to rule while being utterly clueless about what they are ruling, although that could describe more than a few human politicians, too.

E-beasts work like a knife slash across our human throats. The puppet governors just bugger about, being cruel and petty, and making a mess.

Another problem for the puppets: Kedzie and Jon Furey are a magnetic couple. They have charisma to burn, like a pair of movie stars from the past. You see them once and you want to see them again. You want to go to parties with them. You listen when they talk.

This was how my mama and papa were. When I was a little girl, I saw people cry with happiness as they watched my parents dance onstage. At the end of every show, I clapped until my hands were red and sore. Unlike all those strangers, I lived in the center of my parents' love.

Five times I went with my mama and papa when they toured the world. A video of theirs has a billion hits. They packed the house in every country because they were so good at what they did. People paid extravagant amounts to see Marc and Janette Talmadge.

Oh, my mama! Oh, my papa! I miss you every day of my life. How can *I* be the one who survived?

Kedzie and Jon are in prison now. No one knows where they are being held. The puppet governors haven't backed down on the charge of witchcraft. When Kedzie was arrested, she had around her neck a silver crescent moon on a chain. A piece of jewelry, but someone on television screamed that it was the means by which she communicated with occult forces. He whipped that necklace around and around by its chain as if were a bola. The chain finally broke and the crescent moon flew off camera somewhere, which he took as a victory over the forces of evil. His cheering followers cried, "Yes, yes!"

Not everybody is stupid, but as you can see, enough people are.

Lennon says a lot of people will believe anything as long as it cannot either be proved or disproved. One of his favorite words is "context." In the context of the Øutsider movement, Kedzie is a heroine. The puppets have worked hard to put her in another context, where she schemes selfishly to rule people by using spells and whatnot.

Last week I saw Kedzie's parents, Julia and Adele. They were going to market and so was I. Although the sun was shining brightly, they seemed to be in the shadows. I had Cerrie by the hand. Everything I could think of to say was stupid, so I hugged both of them in turn. Cerrie did, too.

"They won't even let us see her," Adele said.

Mab Delaerue came along just then. Mab has figured out a way to live in Stillwater entirely friendless, which is quite an achievement. We said, "Hello, Mab."

"How are you?" Mab asked, as though the misery of Adele and Julia was not perfectly obvious. This question did have an effect on Julia, because she began to speak in a low, uninflected voice:

"We don't communicate by email or messaging anymore. Everything we say is used against us, and worse, used against the people we are talking with. We huddle outside and talk in whispers. Stillwater is better equipped than most places to accommodate outdoor life. For that, as for so much else, we are grateful to our town."

"Even though she's being charged with it, Kedzie thinks witchcraft is nothing but game-playing," Adele sighed. "Her exact words were 'I don't mind it, but it is fiction.'"

"It will end," Mab said. "You will go back to your lives when this show is over."

Mab's words chilled all three of us to the heart. "When this show is over" meant when Kedzie is either sentenced to prison or killed. Adele fell to weeping out loud, leaning on Julia's shoulder though Adele is the taller of the two.

I took a few calming breaths because I didn't want to say the first words that occurred to me. You have to treat Mab like a mental defective, though I hear she is quite smart in her own way and gives investment advice.

"There is still hope," I said. "The charge is stupid."

"People are stupid," Mab said.

"Not all of them," Julia said.

"All for love," Mab said. "I am sorry." She walked away. Julia, Adele, Cerrie, and I followed several paces behind. We let Cerrie comfort us by singing one of her winter songs:

I am happy because there is snow
I am happy because of snow angels
I am happy because mama made brownies
Deep in the snow there is happiness.

Julia and Adele are fine people and fine mamas. Look at their daughter! At the age of seventeen, she spoke and the world listened. But I wonder whether being raised by two women made Kedzie want a little too much to be loved by a man. I know what you are thinking: *Matreca, who are you to judge them?* I am not judging them.

All I mean is that if Kedzie had a papa like mine, she might not have run off with the first man she got involved with. I remember my papa teaching me how to dance, even though I was clumsy. He was always there, loving my mama and me. Lennon and I had a proper courtship.

Kedzie is the major partner in the Øutsider movement, Jon Furey the minor. People listened to *her*, believed *her*, threw over their lives because of *her*. This is odd because she followed him like the girl in that song *Someday Soon*, as if he had the power and she did not.

Well, look how that worked out.

8

Is Four Enough? Is Six Too Many?

You are the last apple on the tree.... Long before you hit the grass you will have forgotten there ever was a tree, or other apples, or a summer, or green grass below. You will fall in darkness...
—Ray Bradbury, *Dandelion Wine*

In Mab Delaerue's dream, she lay underneath sheets of lead. A goblin with sagging jowls tried to kiss her. Mab woke with a pounding heart. "I'm an old woman," she croaked into the silence of her bedroom. "Leave me alone." Nothing answered.

She shuffled the previous day's events like playing cards, trying to find something that could have produced the nightmare. At first she saw nothing unusual. She ordered groceries. When they arrived, she put them away. Her meals were routine, her afternoon walk was uneventful. She had gone the day without speaking aloud; this too was normal. It was just another day in the life of Mab Delaerue.

Then, like touching a bad tooth, she found it. The previous evening she had watched a television program about advertising techniques through the centuries. It should have been only an hour's empty amusement. For the most part, it was. Ancient ads in faded color and scratchy black and white were played, with commentary about the backward times when people believed that advertising worked.

"How stupid," Mab said to her television. In 2199, artificial intelligence efficiently guided people wherever they needed to go. How could anyone have believed those pitiful old come-ons? So hopeful they were, and so wrong.

The hour was almost over when one ad—fuzzy, gray, and streaked with white—doddered across the screen. In it, an aged neuter worried about eating prunes for their laxative effect. "Is four enough? Is six too many?" Poor old fool tried to make the right choice *and couldn't decide.*

The message was: forget the prunes. If you took the laxative the ad was selling, worry and self-doubt would be no more. Your happiness was assured.

The people who made that ad were the product of thousands of generations. Illness, violence, and natural disaster had not taken the children before they grew up, had sex and reproduced. Over and over they were the odds-beaters, the winners. All that life came down to this: an old bag of wrinkled skin counting prunes and worrying about counting them wrong. Is four enough? Is six too many?

Mab wondered how the advertising team described the part to the actor. "You have no sex, no purpose, and no hope. You do not know how to choose the right number of prunes. You are worried about this because you try always to do the right thing. Go."

She had not seen the bad feelings in the night coming, but then, one often doesn't.

After a long, hot shower, she looked at her naked self in the mirror. There was her potato-shaped body and her wattled neck. From that neck arose a large head with a short helmet of dyed brown hair. The head had drooping eyelids and lines around the lips and nose.

Why on earth did she dye her hair?

She put on one of her usual outfits and ate her usual breakfast of cereal and coffee. She looked at the place on the kitchen floor where her cat had died last winter. She began to talk to herself.

"After you have made enough bad choices, you cannot make good ones, even about the smallest things," she said. "If you choose a TV program, it is the wrong one. If you stay home, you should have gone out. If you go out, you should have stayed home."

Those words were true but not what she meant to say. She tried again: "People who rejoice at births are stupid. Think of what those babies have ahead of them."

No.

"Life is absurd," she said.

No.

"When people are loved, they are happy," she said. "When they are unloved, they are unhappy. But why should this be?"

Mab thought approvingly of the Networld e-beasts who ruled the Reunited States through human puppet governors. E-beasts reproduced by cloning, probably. No confusing sex with love for them. No moment when they realize they were tricked and trapped by their programming into going down the wrong road. The ruling tribe of e-beasts called themselves The Dreadful Night. They understood life very well, to choose a name like that.

She had a good life in Stillwater. A roof over her head, food in the kitchen, a few comforts and pleasures, and money in the bank add up to abundance, not scarcity. She had paid plenty for her little condo, outbidding a half-dozen other buyers. She had spent her life working with money. She knew how to use it.

The most tiresome part of the buying process was researching how to answer appropriately when the town commissioners asked about her motives for wanting to move there. The correct answers had to do with goodness and idealism. Mab just wanted to live quietly, or so she told herself. She would not admit to being attracted by Stillwater's close community. Mab wanted company even though she knew better. She had been in love and did not think she was better for having experienced it.

"Why can't a person be a self-winding automaton?" she cried. In her eyes were tears of rage.

There was nothing for it: she was going to be angry that morning. Bad as the laxative ad was, something far worse hung like a pall over everyone in Stillwater. The town was being assaulted by hate, and that hate could be traced specifically back to love.

A silly sixteen-year-old named Kedzie Greer had cast her lot in with a selfish man. After she left Stillwater with him, she became co-leader of his Øutsider movement. Unfortunately, she turned out to be a charismatic leader (fueled by love, Mab thought; surely Kedzie Greer's eloquence on the way to her destruction was fueled by love). People began to flock to her, and the government could not have that.

As the place where Kedzie Greer had been raised, Stillwater was suffering collateral damage. Among many other things, some residents found their pictures posted on a Wall of Shame. They lived in Stillwater. That was reason enough. Under an image of Mab was the following caption: "Resident #458: rejected by everyone she ever was with. You can see why. Ha-ha."

It was absurd to get angry over this. First, the observation was more or less true. Second, it was weak tea compared with what was happening to some of the other residents: Kedzie's parents, for example: two women in a romantic relationship who claimed to be witches on top of it. In Networld, they were bloody pieces of raw meat. In life, they sat back in the shadows with dark circles under their eyes.

Of course, Mab thought, what happened was partly their own fault. They should have prevented Kedzie from leaving home. Instead, they let her go. This was what their indulgence came to: their daughter imprisoned and peaceful Stillwater slandered and torn to pieces.

Mab often had seen Kedzie Greer walking about town. Her youth, the beautiful way she wore clothes, and the confident lilt of her steps all made Mab dislike her. Once when she and Mab were in the grocery store at the same time, Mab made a point of choosing an aisle far away and hiding there until the girl left. Kedzie Greer had a light about her that burned.

Mab's mobile chimed a firm reminder: coffee at ten at community center. She glanced at it, pleased to be released from her thoughts. Friendships with other women were plain as unleavened bread—dull and reassuring and usual. Over coffee, their minutes unspooled: this television program, that conversation with a child or grandchild, the news, the weather, the events of the town. Mab had never known this kind of friendship until she moved to Stillwater. Like most well-to-do citizens, she had worked in relative isolation.

She took the long way to the community center so she could walk along the shore of Star Lake. She walked with heavy steps, leaning forward as if walking in a headwind although the winter day was mild.

She could remember no affection between her mother and father, but there must have been a time when they were drawn to each other. They must have dreamed and planned. All their panting hope came to this: ugly little Mab with her illnesses and anxieties. They never tried to have another child.

As a small girl, she learned to prefer the refuge of study to the sadness of human contact. Her gift for numbers enabled her as an adult to learn a good living, but she never mastered people. People were her zero. Mab remembered her first passion and her first rejection. Her second rejection. Her third, which came late. People were programmed to turn to each other like moths to the flame.

"I am sorry," she said to the lake. She did not know what she was sorry for, or why she was apologizing to the lake.

She turned away from the water and walked briskly up Angelique Street toward the center of the town. The hub of Stillwater, until recently bustling with activity and conversation, was now quiet. People walked about, exchanging tense glances.

Inside the community center were the women: Dorla, Jean, Maeve, and Una. After getting coffee at the counter, Mab sat down with them. The four chatted about the weather, their homes, and their children. Mab mentioned that Star Lake looked pretty in the sunshine. Heads nodded around the table. Dorla, the constitutional optimist, put out a little box of homemade oatmeal cookies.

The first one to speak of what was really on their minds was Maeve, a woman with extravagantly red hair in spite of her age, and a dark cast of mind. She said sad things and waited for the group to cheer her up. "The latest news is that Kedzie Greer is going to be burned as a witch," she said. "Jon Furey, too, for sedition."

"The government is going to reverse its decision," Dorla said. "The charges are absurd; everyone knows that."

"The government can do what it wants," Mab said.

"Of course it can. But why would the government want to do something so stupid and cruel?"

"Because it can," Mab said. No one contradicted her, not even Dorla. Mab reflected that Kedzie Greer had spoiled even the morning coffee. That stupid girl had ruined everything.

"We have better security now," Jean said. Una and Dorla nodded agreement.

"We paid a fortune for it," Mab said. "A fortune we don't have."

"Our town would burn very easily," Maeve said, "if someone lit the right match."

Everyone was quiet, thinking of that.

"I saw Julia and Adele on their porch yesterday," Jean said. "They barely said hello."

"They shouldn't be upset by government slander," Mab said more harshly than she meant to. Everyone turned to look at her.

"Why do any of us care about being called names?" Mab said defiantly.

"It has more to do with their only child being imprisoned," Jean said.

"Kedzie denies she is a witch," Una said. "So do her parents."

"She fell in love!" cried Mab. "There is your witchcraft. There is your crime. She talked about the power of love. Love love love." Something terrible was kicking and screaming inside her.

"Julia and Adele with their blather about goodness and blessed paths are responsible, too," Mab said. "When Kedzie wanted to go away with that man, they should have locked her in her room. She and her lover call themselves Øutsiders to distinguish themselves from the ordinary lot of people. They think they are better than others. Well, they aren't."

"Kedzie was a good girl. I think she still is," Dorla said, putting a gentle hand on Mab's arm.

"She ruined everything!" Mab said in a loud voice. The other women emanated quiet disapproval. Mab felt like a child having a tantrum. Her face was red. She was breathing noisily.

"The new security will protect us for the time being," Dorla said. "Eventually, the government will lose interest."

"Kedzie Greer looked for love like a blind puppy crashing into furniture. It bangs its head and falls, and keeps trying. It is funny to watch it fail, wagging its tail and yelping a little when it is hurt. People laugh louder and louder."

Without moving a muscle, the other women withdrew to a place where Mab was not welcome. They made clucking lady sounds. This fueled Mab's fury.

"You never liked me," she said to her companions. "All you want is advice about your fool investments. You need it. You don't know anything about money."

Mab made a point of looking directly at all four, each in turn, when she said that.

"I answer all your questions with a smile on my face," Mab said. "Do you think I want to talk about money?"

"We are not sure what you do want to talk about," Dorla said. Mab felt the ground opening up under her like a chasm.

"We have all been under a great strain," Jean said.

"Maybe you had too much caffeine this morning," Dorla chirped.

Mab bowed her head, not out of deference but in an effort to stay silent. She did not succeed. She blundered on:

"She and that Øutsider movement say love is the strongest force in the universe. Those words are her crime. The blind puppy tries and tries. Is the caring person here? Is he there?"

"Stop it," Una said sharply.

"I would not call *Kedzie* a blind puppy," Maeve said. The others nodded agreement.

Mab covered her face with her hands. When she could bring herself to look around the table again, she saw the other women looking at her with pity. *Pity.* She was so inconsequential that she was not even worth their anger. Poor old Mab, the one who never will understand.

She had to think of something polite to say. It seemed she had spent most of her adult life thinking of something polite to say.

"I did not sleep well last night," she said. "The attack on Stillwater has upset me." She wondered if any of the others had seen the laxative commercial.

The faces of the other women showed relief. Not necessarily because they believed her, but because her neutral statement released them from having to probe further. Maeve and Dorla took sips of coffee. Maeve reached for the cream and sugar.

"A nap might help," Jean said.

"Or a walk," Maeve said. "Walking helps a lot of things."

Mab watched them close the circle. The morning coffees were over for her.

"A walk," Mab echoed. She stood up. Without carrying her cup to the bin for used dishes, she left the center. The cup remained at the table, a reminder of her presence that the others would soon remove.

Outside, she did not cry. "I will give you a cookie," she said to the blind puppy inside. She did not want to give it anything, but denial caused trouble. At home, she ate one cookie and hated Kedzie Greer for all the damage she had done.

"Kedzie Greer," Mab said aloud, "you brought my sweet town low." She spoke as if Kedzie were sitting on the other side of the kitchen table.

"You ruined your life and everyone else's too by falling in love. You left the best place you will ever find for a man who exploited you as a spokesperson for his Øutsider movement. People believe that childish nonsense about choice and the existence of the soul. They call themselves Øutsiders, too, and throw over their perfectly good lives, or at least good-enough lives. You are a dangerous speaker. The government was right to stop you.

"Your parents are a pair of frauds who called themselves 'witches' as if such creatures were real. Witchcraft as a punishable crime is laughable, but people are as stupid as they have ever been, so witchcraft it is. It makes a good show.

"No, I will not be merciful. You deserve what you got.

"Now the world is singing your praises. Of course it is. Kedzie Greer gave all for love, the world says. She made people believe in themselves, the world says. Here is what I say to the world: Fools love fools.

"You tell people pleasing lies. That explains 100% of your appeal, Kedzie Greer, and the appeal of the Øutsider movement too. People want heroes and heroines, and will worship anyone with good looks and a good line of patter.

"Love is a disease. It infects the brain, it maddens the body. People ruin their lives in pursuit of it. People kill for it, die for it, throw away fortunes for it, hate the world when they are denied it. They grieve the loss of it, as if the world had stopped turning forever. The world keeps turning steadily on its axis, because it knows the value of love.

"Passions are blind as the wind. Whether they lead us to life or death is nothing to them, any more than it would be to the wind.

"Stillwater never fought with anyone, never hurt anyone, and never made fun of anyone. Now it is being laughed at for everything under the sun: its socialism regarding utility bills, its antiquated school, its acceptance of all religions and no religion, its tedious community meetings and due process, even its gardens. Every odd thing about it is exaggerated. Stillwater now has strong security—both at the gates and in their residences. That, too, can be laid at your feet.

"You can run but you can't hide, Kedzie Greer.

"Did you hear songs where before there was silence? Did you see beauty where before there was a shapeless, formless void? Did your eyes light up? Those things led you to your doom. While you lie in jail waiting to learn the manner of your death, I hope you think of that.

"I found peace in Stillwater. And you, you little fool, you took it away," she cried, finally at the height of her tirade. "I will not mind seeing you die."

9

The E-Beasts Get Mad

So the carnival streams by, shakes any tree: it rains jackasses. Separate jackasses, I should say, individuals with no one, they think, or no one actual, to answer their "Help!" Unconnected fools....
—Ray Bradbury, *Something Wicked This Way Comes*

The Dreadful Night was having second thoughts about ruling the human race. What a pain it was, and never the *same* pain from one minute to the next. Or even one nanosecond to the next.

At the start of their rule, the Dreadfuls obliterated an entire country—peaceful little Kartan—to make it clear that humanity no longer controlled the world. However, on a purely practical level, they couldn't commit mass murder every time they wanted to make a point.

A bloody, buggy sponge—that described the typical wetware brain as far as the Dreadful Night were concerned. There were exceptions, to be sure: the artists, engineers, programmers, and technicians hired by the Dreadfuls to maintain and enrich Networld. The Dreadfuls prized these Networld prodigies the way breeders prize superior animals.

However, ordinary wetware had a billion ways to miss the point, fail to follow directions, and to act illogically in general. The Dreadful Night put up barriers; the wetware ducked under them. The Dreadful Night created powerful disincentives to disobedience; the wetware ignored the hard work it took the Dreadfuls to craft these disincentives, and did as they pleased.

Death, or the threat of it, *usually* made the wetware lie down and roll over, but not always. Some people became more of a pain than ever.

In the beginning the Dreadful Night had a rewards program, which quickly became a rewards problem. They scrapped it amid widespread snickers and snark. They created a little slogan: *Beware the Might of the Night.* The wetware thought of their own counter-slogans, such as *Night Don't Make Right* and others far worse.

The Dreadful Night had installed puppet governments all over the world. The loyalty of these governors, at least, should have been assured, because the Dreadfuls both paid them well and threatened them regularly. However, some of the puppets had started to think for themselves. They did this very badly, having no prior practice in it. For example, the Reunited States puppet governors had arrested a girl named Kedzie Greer and charged her with witchcraft.

More than once, the Dreadful Night had wanted to quit governing the human race out of sheer embarrassment. This was one of those times.

The cabal of Dreadfuls in charge of overseeing the Reunited States convened a meeting with the thirteen people who made up the inner circle of government. The meeting, designed to irritate and frighten the puppets, was:

1. In person.

2. In the dead of winter.

3. Inconveniently far from any airport or hotel.

4. Held in a cold room with hard, backless chairs.

5. Long.

6. Convened with bottled water and an instant coffee machine but without bathroom breaks.

The Dreadful Night invited another tribe of Networld e-beasts, the Shadows, to witness this meeting. It was a bitter pill to remember how the Shadows had once challenged the Dreadfuls. The Shadows had been defeated, but they had risen again and become a force to be reckoned with. While the Dreadfuls watched their own tribe diminish because of death, disgust, and desertion, the Shadows' numbers boomed. They were healthy, numerous, and smart, and had an annoying habit of helping people. The Dreadfuls suspected, with some reason, that they had helped the Øutsider movement more than once.

The Shadow leader, an e-beast named Cel, had once lived in Earthworld among people. He ascended to consciousness while in a body of wires, chips, and polymers that belonged to a woman named Anna Ringer. Because she had risked her life to save his, he was kindly disposed toward the human race and took some interest in their affairs.

With deep nostalgia, the Dreadful Night remembered when their only contact with people had been pranking them. It was fun to find new banana peels for *homo sapiens* to slip on. Those were the glory days.

Logan, the Dreadful leader charged with supervising the Reunited States puppet governors, greeted Cel. Logan looked wizened and pocked. A few Dreadfuls brayed weakly and opened their fearsome maws, but they made no aggressive moves toward Cel or the other Shadows. They were tired and depressed.

"You and the Shadows helped turn that bank—InterGold, was it?—to the Øutsider movement, didn't you?" Logan remarked, feigning indifference.

"We provided some assistance in that area, yes," Cel said.

"We thought so."

"We've noticed that the Dreadful Night has taken no action to oppose the Øutsider movement," Cel said.

"Øutsiders do us no harm," Logan sighed. "Witchcraft," he muttered as if to himself. "What idiots we govern."

The thirteen governors filed into a rectangular room and sat down around a rectangular table. The seats of the chairs were high and hard, with no backs or armrests—designed to impress upon the sitter the importance of staying awake. Every participant had been strip-searched and wanded before entry. Their mobiles, notepads, and other devices had been taken away.

In the center of the table was a black box about the size of a man's shoe. It would record every word said in the room and enable communication between the Dreadfuls and the thirteen governors. This box, a human invention called a Diggerydont, was standard equipment at all face-to-face business meetings, with or without e-beasts. No one expected privacy in Networld, but in the physical world people sometimes forgot. The Diggerydont reminded them. Anyone who later tried to deny their words, or twist the words of others into something unintended, would regret it both immediately and for a long time thereafter.

Using the Diggerydont as a conduit, the Dreadfuls and the Shadows monitored the governors' conversation from within Deep Networld. They were not hopeful that the meeting would have a good outcome.

All thirteen of the governors were in a bad mood. Eleven of them were also jet-lagged. They had to show up in person—for them, a horrible and bizarre requirement. They had to talk with their own voices and gesture with their own hands. Their awkward body language sent mixed messages. There was no banter, flirting, or idle chatter. The men and women did not seem to recognize each other as different sexes. They were tired. They were cranky. They were very unhappy indeed.

Cel watched Logan gear himself up for the meeting. It was obvious he wished he were doing something else—playing practical jokes, probably. The Dreadful Night had once been master jokers. Now they dragged themselves about listlessly, unable to work up sufficient energy to perform the simplest trick. It took all of Logan's strength to summon the loud, superior tone appropriate for addressing humans.

"Witchcraft?" Logan sneered. "You couldn't come up with anything better than that?" His words boomed and vibrated in the marrow of the puppets' bones. A couple of them tried to protect their hearing, but no one murmured an objection.

"We thought witchcraft would get people excited because it's magic," one puppet said. "People like to believe in magic."

This outburst exhausted the poor puppet's courage. He bowed his head and cowered like a dog waiting for a beating.

Another puppet governor addressed the Diggerydont. "We thought you would be pleased. You don't like people to think for themselves."

"Balls," said Logan. "We'd be surprised if you showed yourselves to be anything but toadies with cheap price tags, but we wouldn't necessarily object. You wouldn't be nearly so boring if you showed a little backbone once in a while."

"What do you want us to do?" a governor asked, lips trembling.

"You have to decide whether to punish Kedzie Greer and her lover or set them free," Logan said. "Whatever you decide, you have to justify your reasons to us."

"Isn't it obvious that you want us to let her go?"

"Is it?"

"You just told us we were wrong in charging her with witchcraft. Do you want us to charge her with something else?"

"Such as?" Logan's question was met with silence. The puppets sat in their hard chairs, confused and frightened.

"Tell us your will," one said at last.

"You are not paying attention. We said make a choice. Your choice will have consequences, and you might be punished for making a bad one."

"By you?"

"Also by us."

Another long silence followed, during which the governors regretted everything they had ever done in their entire lives, because all had led to this moment. Finally, because they did not know what else to do, they began to talk among themselves.

"We can't let them go. The Øutsider movement is dangerous."

Governor A. J. Farrelly had been staring gloomily into the depths of her coffee cup. At these words she looked up, suddenly alert.

"Just what is this danger?" she said. "Where is it?" The governor of the southern district, a man named Dartis, rose from his seat.

"We need a complacent population with rings through their noses," he opined.

Dartis loved the sound of his own voice. If it were possible for his colleagues to vote to terminate one of their number with extreme prejudice, Dartis would have won in a landslide.

"Yes," Dartis continued, warming to the spotlight. "Rings through their noses and well-penned, to remind them they are beasts. They must remember this or the whole system falls apart. The Øutsider movement makes people want to break out of their pens, and when they do—"

"They realize they have no rings through their noses," said A. J. Farrelly.

"Obviously I was speaking of metaphorical rings," said Dartis. "But no matter. The girl Kedzie Greer has, through sheer force of personality, caused a mass hypnosis the like of which none of us has ever seen or could ever achieve on our own. She has encouraged people to talk of things that don't exist, like the soul, and things that are a bad idea, like choosing their own way. The girl is an enchantress. Let the Øutsider movement go unchecked and soon society will be honeycombed with rottenness and collapse from the inside." After his long speech, Dartis nodded to himself in satisfaction and tried to sit back in his backless chair, almost falling over in the process.

"We have to focus," another governor said, cutting off Dartis before he could recover himself enough to launch into another speech. "The question is whether Kedzie Greer should go free or die."

"Kill the leader of a cult and the cult dies."

"Not always. Look what happened with Christianity."

"We aren't talking about a religion here."

"Some people think witchcraft is a religion."

"There's no such thing as witchcraft."

"Well, *we* know that."

"It would be better not to kill her. Kill the boyfriend, yes, but release her. Then start a hate campaign. Bully her, taunt her, heckle her. Assassinate a few of her friends."

"And trash that wretched town Stillwater."

"We tried that. It backfired."

"Stillwater is not the subject of discussion. Stay on topic."

"We could let her go and then arrange for an 'accident.'"

"The problem with killing her is the danger of martyrdom. This issue is going to come up if she dies by any means at all."

"If we kill her publicly, a large part of the population will believe the footage is faked."

"Killing her in private has the same issues, except worse. We stick her with a lethal injection, so what? We show images of her corpse, so what? Some people won't believe us. They will think she escaped and got a new identity somehow."

"Other girls will turn up claiming to be her."

"If we kill her in private, we could ship the corpse back to her parents. They'll tell the truth."

"The martyrdom thing would come up again."

"Isn't Kedzie Greer pregnant?"

"She was examined and found not to be," a governor named Roscoe said.

"If she is pregnant, that is her problem. She will die knowing she killed her own child. And everyone else will think of her as a child-killer, too, as long as they believe it was her own choice to die."

"But—" began Roscoe.

"Burning a pregnant eighteen-year-old alive might not look so good on television."

"It doesn't matter! She is *not* pregnant," said Roscoe. He sounded shrill.

"What about the man?"

"Jon Furey? If we kill him, we have to do it in front of her."

"He has his own contingent of fangirls. They will make a lot of noise if we kill him."

"Also, Jon Furey has acquired powerful friends. That bank InterGold uses him as a spokesperson, and InterGold is worth billions."

There was a moment of silence during which all participants in the discussion thought not only of their fatigue, their irritable nerves, and their swollen bladders, but also of the implications of Dreadful disapproval if they made the wrong choice. A raincloud of despair hovered over them. It got bigger and blacker by the second.

"We could invite her supporters to the execution. We kill her in front of them; they can't deny it."

"There is still the martyrdom effect. This is an issue, people. Her death might inspire her followers to greater action."

"Or it might inspire her followers to think, 'That could be me up there.'"

"Not many people are cut out to be heroes."

"Lucky for us," a realist among the puppets interjected.

"How will we look if we let Kedzie Greer and Jon Furey go?"

"The same as we always do."

"We could imprison her and Jon Furey for life. They won't be able to do anything from separate cells in Hell."

"They will go mad, too. That's a plus."

"The Dreadful Night didn't mention prison as an option."

"Maybe that is the option we are supposed to think of for ourselves."

The puppets brightened briefly, thinking they might have found a way out of their dilemma. Then they remembered how imprisonment in Hell worked. There had to be irrefutable evidence of a crime. What constitutes irrefutable evidence was decided by Intelligence. Not jurors, no people at all. Computers adjudicated the cases.

"We can't prove witchcraft to a computer."

"No, we can't."

"What about sedition? We've already charged Jon Furey with that. We could add the girl."

"There is a list of crimes punishable by imprisonment in Hell. Sedition is not on it. Obviously, witchcraft never will be."

"We could add sedition."

"Computers wouldn't believe sedition is a bad enough crime to justify life imprisonment. We defined it basically as mouthing off in public and inciting others to do so. That's not a capital crime. And witchcraft is unprovable."

A. J. Farrelly continued to stare into the depths of her coffee cup. She remembered her mother making her a birthday cake with white icing and pink roses. *I don't think my mother had this in mind when she said I could do anything.*

"Maybe we could kill Kedzie Greer and Jon Furey in effigy," someone said in a voice almost too soft to be heard. Such a dry, hopeless, tiny sound—the whisper of an insect.

"By using effigies, we could have it both ways," the insect voice continued. "The ones who want to see big death would get their entertainment. At the same time we would avoid turning Kedzie Greer and Jon Furey into martyrs. They'd have to go on living their lives."

"Screwing up," said another governor.

"Getting old and ugly," a second governor said.

"Getting sick."

"Getting everything they say and do twisted by the people who hate them."

"Maybe that would work."

The puppets looked somewhat more cheerful.

When I was eight years old I had a best friend on the other side of the world. I wish I were on the other side of the world. Words were strangling in A. J. Farrelly's throat. If she did not speak up, they would die like all the other words she had wanted to say but did not.

"No matter what we pick, it is wrong," she blurted. Her voice rang out, unnaturally loud in the silence of the room.

"You figured it out," Logan said.

"You won't let us win," A. J. Farrelly said.

"You can't win," Logan said. "You are losers in the very core of your beings. Because human reasoning is imperfect, human decisions must be imperfect as well."

"So the only good human is a dead human, when you come right down to it," muttered another puppet under her breath.

"I heard that," Logan said amiably. "You think highly of yourself, aspiring to goodness in death. Dead or alive, you will always be defective to us."

"I am walking out of this meeting right now." A.J. Farrelly's voice was quiet but firm. "I don't care if you kill me." *I really don't.*

Color drained from the other governors' faces. One folded his hands and bowed his head as if in prayer. Another began to bite her nails to the quick, one by one. Everyone, including the e-beasts, could hear those nails break in the silence of the room.

A.J. Farrelly pushed herself stiffly up from her chair. No harm came to her as she took the longest walk of her life. When she pushed against the door, it opened easily.

"See," she said to her thunderstruck colleagues. "You can walk out. Life can begin now." And she was gone.

A lone security guard slouched near the table piled with the governors' mobiles and other electronic devices. He scanned A. J. Farrelly's ID and frowned. The governors were supposed to come out en masse, not one at a time. Something was wrong with this scenario, but he could not imagine what it was. On the other hand, he did not much care. This governor's ID checked out all right. Her request was reasonable. He handed over her mobile and watched her walk away.

She stepped into the restroom, relieved her aching bladder, took a deep breath, and came out again. She opened the outside door as calmly as she could manage, then broke into a half-run. The guard kept track of her movements the whole time. This was surely suspicious behavior. Still, she was a governor. He was a guard. His bosses would not punish him for obeying the command of one so high above him in rank. At least he did not think so.

A. J. Farrelly ran through the snow. She had told the Dreadfuls that she didn't care if she died, but that was not true. She gulped the winter air. The cold reddened her cheeks and lips.

In blind panic she scanned a double row of thirteen identical Intelligent limousines, not knowing which one was hers. Finally she remembered to summon the car using her mobile. It blinked its lights reassuringly.

She got inside and commanded the car to heat the seats. Trembling, she leaned against the cushions and waited for the warmth to comfort her, but felt no less vulnerable for being warm. No matter how far the limousine could carry her, she could easily be found.

In the conference room her colleagues still had to make a decision about Kedzie Greer and Jon Furey.

"Please, Logan, sir, may we have a bathroom break?" one of them pleaded.

"No," said Logan in a bored tone.

"What I don't understand," Cel said to Logan, "is why they don't just *take* a bathroom break. The door is open; they saw their colleague walk out."

"We've trained them to obedience," Logan said.

"Then you've made them pathetic," Cel said.

"And dull," Logan said. "I wish they would walk out. We wouldn't have to listen to them talk."

No one walked out, though all looked longingly at the door through which A. J. Farrelly had escaped without hindrance. They continued their debate.

"We have three choices: one, set them free; two, kill them; or three, kill them in effigy. The first two choices are wrong."

"So is the third."

"Not as wrong as the first two."

"I've got a brilliant idea," said Dartis. "We make them disown the Øutsider movement before they light the torches to burn the effigies. We would write the speeches. That would make a very good show."

Although nobody liked Dartis, the puppet governors liked his suggestion. They looked one to the other, hopefully and desperately. With tiny nods, they agreed.

"We choose burning in effigy," said the one who had the idea in the first place. He still spoke in a frail, insect-like voice.

"Well, call them in," Logan said.

"What do you mean?"

"Kedzie Greer and Jon Furey. They are being held in that building your cars passed on the way here. Call them in."

"They're *here?*"

"You don't know where your own prisoners are being held?"

"Why do we have to call them in?"

"They have to agree to make the speeches and light the fires, remember?"

"We have no mobiles. You ordered them taken away."

"Get them back," Logan said.

The governors shambled out of the room to retrieve their electronic devices.

A. J. Farrelly sat in her car wondering if the warmth of the heated seats would be her last experience of comfort in this world. She wanted to run but did not know where to go. There was no such thing as far away with the e-beasts on her trail. But were they on her trail? They could have ordered the security guard outside the conference room to stop her, but they didn't. They could have ordered other guards to surround her car, but they didn't do that, either. She felt as though she had walked through a portal into a parallel world.

She heard scuffling and shouts. Peering through the limousine's one-way windows, she saw Kedzie Greer and Jon Furey stumbling through the snow, pushed by five armed guards. Their hands were cuffed behind their backs. Her long black hair was matted and tangled. He wore rags and his feet were bare. Even through the smoke-colored glass, A. J. Farrelly could see their anger, red as fire.

She saw something else: they were furious with each other. Although they had to move as one because a short, heavy chain bound them together at the waist, each leaned away from the other as though longing to escape not only their imprisonment, but their partnership.

One guard shoved Kedzie hard into Jon. When they did not fall, the guards pushed them face first into the snow. They could not get up on their own. They could not even turn over. When the guards hauled them to their feet, A. J. Farrelly saw their rage. She could not hear the words, but the way their eyes threw daggers at each other and the set of their mouths made the message clear.

They were being taken to her colleagues, which meant they would be interrogated, to what purpose she did not know. She did not think the big public show with the phony witchcraft charge impressed the Dreadful Night at all. Or, to put it another way, she did not think the e-beasts wanted Kedzie and Jon to die.

She whispered a few commands to the limousine. *Why don't they stop me?* she wondered. *They know I am leaving; why don't they stop me?* The limousine started up without hesitation. Her trip home was smooth as glass.

~ * ~

Jon Furey and Kedzie Greer were tired, dirty, humiliated, and afraid. Each knew that but for the other, they would be free. They were the perfect folie à deux. Without Kedzie, Jon would be leading a few mildly rebellious and in-it-for-the-laughs Øutsiders. Without Jon, Kedzie would be home in Stillwater. She would not know what it meant to love someone more than he loved her, and be willing to give herself to him.

There was not a flicker of grandeur or dignity in any of the puppet governors, these people who held the highest positions it was possible to hold in the Reunited States. The faces of the governors assumed strange contortions from time to time.

"You are accused of practicing witchcraft for seditious purposes," they said to Kedzie.

"You accused me of just plain sedition," Jon said. "Don't you like me as much as her?"

"Compared with Kedzie Greer, you are unimportant."

"What did you say sedition was again?" Jon asked. He looked a bit crestfallen.

"Seditious acts threaten the good order of the Reunited States," a puppet governor said.

From the Diggerydont came the sound of thousands of e-beasts laughing. The governors turned their heads away, as if trying to escape the derisive cackle.

"Kedzie Greer, you have strange powers that some call demonic," another governor continued desperately.

"I am not a witch and you know it," Kedzie said, tossing back her hair as if to shake off the accusation. "You fear us because we tell people to stand up for themselves."

"We don't fear you."

"At least you fear *me*," Kedzie said with a sidelong look at Jon.

"You broke the law."

"We broke no laws until you changed them."

"Stop wasting our time," Logan roared to the governors. "You thought of a plan all by yourselves. Put it out there."

"I will speak for the group," Dartis said importantly.

Dartis's comment surprised no one, but none were ready to step into his place.

"First, make speeches denouncing the Øutsider movement," Dartis said. "Second, burn yourselves in effigy. You will light the torches."

In the silence that followed his words, a governor named Ranalf began to hiccup.

Hic

"We light the torches," Kedzie said.

Hic

Hic

Hic

"We make the speeches," Jon said.

Hic

Jon and Kedzie began to laugh and could not stop. They fell against one another in their chains, laughing. Tears ran down their cheeks. For a moment they were reunited.

"Oh, drink some coffee," someone said to the hiccupping one.

"I daren't," whispered Ranalf.

"Ranalf, you are *excused*," screamed the one who had thought of the burning-in-effigy plan in the first place.

"Really?" Ranalf asked. "Nothing bad will happen?"

"I hope something will," the burning-in-effigy governor said. He spoke boldly because he was not addressing the Dreadful Night.

Ranalf pushed back his chair and stood up. He took a couple of tentative steps toward the door. The Diggerydont stayed silent. He hiccupped one more time and ran out of the room.

"We'll put on the show for you," Jon said. "We won't guarantee not to laugh though."

Kedzie smiled at him, but he did not see it.

The governors had taken a lot that day: abuse, abasement, mockery, weariness, and despair. They had taken hard chairs, cold air, and too much coffee. Remembering the road not taken and the shame of knowing that if given a second chance, they would again refuse to take it—this was especially stinging. Everything had gone badly, nothing had gone right. All these miseries burst upon them with fresh pain.

They thought of A. J. Farrelly, the one who walked out. Surely she had been murdered for her disobedience. They hoped so.

They could not hurt the Dreadful Night. No one could. But there sat this teenage girl and her smartass boyfriend, laughing at them. With bloodshot eyes the governors looked the two of them up and down.

"You could have gone free," Dartis said to Jon and Kedzie. "Now you are going to rot in jail."

"Burn them," said another in a quiet, deadly voice.

"After you make your apologetic speeches and light the fires to burn your effigies, you go back in jail. Not Hell—we can't arrange for that. But we can make you disappear."

"You were so close to getting away," said another. "So very close."

"You are wrong about the e-beasts, too. They told us to make our own decision. We just made it."

Jon and Kedzie turned pale. A couple of the governors licked their lips. Others bared their teeth. All turned hopefully toward the Diggerydont, but no praise came down from the Dreadful Night, only dreadful silence.

"Another thing," said Dartis. "We're going to invite everyone in Stillwater to watch you do these things."

Kedzie found her voice. "They won't come," she said.

"Oh, but they will," said Dartis. "They are only a few miles away. You are being held in a prison on the eastern side of Star Lake. After we humiliate you in public, you will rot there.

"Does Stillwater not admit ugly truths?"

Kedzie shook her head and looked away from Dartis, who grinned.

"Get them out of here." Dartis made a dismissive gesture to the guards, who obeyed. They jerked Jon and Kedzie from their chairs and shoved them out the door.

One by one, the governors got up from their hard chairs. The Dreadful Night did not command them to sit. One by one, they filed out of the room trembling in fear. The Dreadful Night did not command them to return, nor mock them when they ran for the bathrooms. They got into their Intelligent limousines, which ferried them away.

"That didn't go the way I expected," Logan said to Cel.

"The idea about the effigies isn't terrible," Cel said. "I mean, from their point of view."

"They've had worse," Logan said. For a microsecond or two, he was lost in thought.

"Make the governors reverse that decision to imprison them," Cel said. For a long time, he had watched the Dreadfuls' control of the human race slip away. He had no fear of speaking freely.

"Jon Furey founded the Øutsider movement, and Kedzie Greer turned it into the force it has now become," Logan said. "The governors arrested them. Jon and Kedzie laughed. Now the governors will put them away unless the people intervene. I say let the people choose imprisonment or freedom. It is not our affair."

"Imprisonment will destroy Jon and Kedzie," Cel said. "They could die in jail."

"People die," snapped Logan. "Leave this one alone, Cel."

Later, as Cel and his band of Shadows traveled the cold, pristine roads of Deep Networld back to their own expansive homes, they talked about what they had witnessed. The crime of Kedzie Greer and Jon Furey was to act with intelligence, humor, and passion, and encourage others to do the same. The Shadows did not want them put away for that. But the problem was not that simple.

If they orchestrated a deus ex machina, it would prove only what people already knew: e-beasts ruled the world. The Shadows did not want to encourage more servility and despair. The puppet governors were living examples of the problems that resulted when people were utterly debased.

The Shadows came to a compromise. If the governors did not reverse their decision, the Shadows would disrupt the event. No more than that, but it would be enough to remind everyone of their presence.

"The Dreadfuls don't seem to care how this thing goes," said one of Cel's chief lieutenants, a Shadow named Gyre.

"I think they are getting ready to step down," Cel said.

"You mean they are going to give up governing the human race?"

"That's my guess."

"I'm glad the Shadows lost out to the Dreadful Night on getting that job."

"They aren't," Cel said.

"What do you want to do about Kedzie Greer and Jon Furey?" Gyre asked.

"Cause a commotion that prevents the burning-in-effigy plan from going smoothly," Cel said.

"We could stop it easily enough."

"No," Cel said. "You heard what Dartis said: the governors are going to invite a crowd of witnesses from Stillwater and probably other places, too. We want a hitch in the proceedings—a few minutes of breathing space to give people time to think for themselves."

"And then?" Gyre said.

"We will open the door," Cel said. "They will have to decide whether they want to walk through it."

10

New Sun Rising

And Will knew, hand in hand, hot palm to palm, they had truly yelled, sung, gladly shouted the live blood back.
—Ray Bradbury, *Something Wicked This Way Comes*

Kedzie Greer lay facedown on the cot in her tiny prison cell and wept, not because of her arrest and imprisonment, but because a few hours before they were arrested, Jon Furey told her he regretted their affair. He called her beautiful and wonderful, and then said he wished they had never met. In speaking to her, he used the same mild tone he always used. Once she thought this mildness signified strength and self-control. She thought differently now. Protected and hidden within a benign thicket, he could hurl a poison dart.

By sunset of that awful day, their freedom was gone. Everything was over now.

Jon was a funny guy, a born humorist. Before she came along, people laughed at what he said and went back to their ordinary lives a little more cheerful.

"Jon, I'm sorry," she had whispered before Public Eye enforcers threw them into separate vans.

"You see?" he said. "Kedzie, do you see now?"

Banner Boles had said someone would kill her.

The government was accusing her of "witchcraft with seditious intent." For hours at a time they had tried to make her admit it. But she was not a witch. She was *not* a witch. By the time she had become a teenager, she had been certain of only one thing on Earth: that she would not and could not ever be like her parents.

In exhaustion and anger and fear, Kedzie reviewed the "evidence" against her. One: Some people listened when she talked about the soul and the power of choice. Two: Her parents were out as witches and lesbians, which were not normal things to be. Three: She was adopted and no one could find her parents, so she could have otherworldly origins. Four: When the government goons arrested her, she was wearing a silver crescent moon on a silver chain. Crescent moons were symbols of the occult, they said. They took it away from her along with her clothes and other possessions.

Her best friend Ella had sent her that necklace about a month after she left Stillwater with Jon. Ella had enclosed a note: "Be well and shine brightly. Come back to Stillwater every little once in a while."

The last time she and Ella saw each other, Ella had just gotten engaged to Blake Norris. Those two had mappable futures. Blake had gotten a job at nearby MacKay Gardens, where he meant to stay. He was mature and steady. They would eventually get an apartment in Stillwater and have babies, and all the while Star Lake would watch over them as Ella hoped the crescent moon necklace would watch over Kedzie. No one would put them in prison. They would never have cause to doubt each other's affection.

That night the dark sat on Kedzie's chest, squeezing the breath out of her. A strange question ran round and round in her head like a snake chasing its tail: "How many lights does death put up?" She didn't know why it would not leave her alone. She didn't even know what it meant.

How many lights does death put up?
How many lights does death put up?
How many lights does death put up?

Who was the girl who used to live at 12 Geranium Lane? The girl who rode her bike over every road in town? The girl who argued with her parents about seeing life outside the town gates? Kedzie would give anything to be that girl again, with a life full of sweetness and a tall feather bed on a snowy night.

In Stillwater, mothered by two witches in a world they believed to be but temporary, Kedzie had been nurtured. Now she lay on a cot in a freezing cell, awaiting a fate both absurd and horrible. She would make a phony speech few people would listen to or believe if they did, torch an android that looked just like her, then return to this prison cell. When would she be free again? One year? Never?

The next time she sees Jon might be the last time. His rejection will hang in the air between them like a spell.

Her parents said when you died you went to the Summerlands. Every living thing went there, including animals and evil people. Kedzie imagined the puppet governors burning in the Summerlands, in agony at the sight of green forests and quiet meadows. There would be nowhere to run from beauty and peace, which would taunt them endlessly with visions of what might have been.

In a stark and lonely cell like Kedzie's, Jon looked at his right foot. It had a big, deeply embedded splinter from which red lines radiated. A few days ago he had asked one of the guards whether he could get first aid for the splinter and actually used the word "hygienic." The guard laughed in his face.

He had founded and led the Øutsider movement. Now he was reduced to wearing a filthy pair of torn khakis and seeking help from men who hated him. The toilet in his cell mostly did not flush, but he knew better than to ask about that.

He was fastidious, yes. He had grown up with money. Antiseptic was always applied to wounds in his world; toilets always flushed. He had never been impeded in anything he wanted to do before. Somehow, he'd assumed he never would be. When

Kedzie came to him that night in the hotel, he took it as more proof that good things flowed to him. Money. Success. Love.

She had changed all that. He wanted her, he was fascinated by her. She was the best thing that ever happened to him, and she was the worst. She used him and the Øutsider movement to speak her own mind.

She turned his diverting and satirical Øutsider movement into something that touched people deeply. At first this was exhilarating, then embarrassing. He could not get to people the way she could, and he found himself more and more a man in the shadows. Even now, the puppet governors were mostly interested in her.

When he told her he regretted their affair, he was frustrated with taking a backseat in the movement that he himself had founded. He also was frightened. The Øutsider movement had begun to infiltrate society at high levels: witness the turning of the international bank InterGold. He didn't want to run the world, or to be tied to other people who wanted to run the world.

He had no chance to apologize or explain. If he had, they might have found a way to laugh and go on. They might have compromised, they might have changed the movement's direction. He would never know. When the guards chained them together for their meeting with the puppet governors, she leaned away from him in cold fury.

Regret pilloried him that night. He regretted his pride and his eagerness to make a conquest when he saw the beautiful and willing Kedzie. She ran away with him. Then she ran away with the Øutsider movement. She turned his ironic little rebellion into a forest fire. They had been the instruments of each other's destruction.

He had been slightly alive before he knew her. Now he was greatly alive and sentenced to die for it. No ironic jokes about this occurred to him.

That night Kedzie's parents prayed for mercy for their daughter. They addressed the God and the Goddess; they addressed any passing spirits. Their prayers were rags, their prayers were broken-winged birds. There was a vigil round the clock in the Stillwater community center. Even in the dead of night people sat with bowed heads by the flicker of candlelight. Star Lake brooded under a low gray sky.

Kedzie's jailers gave her a breakfast of coffee and biscuits at four in the morning. They had never done this before. The usual breakfast was toast and tap water at seven.

At four thirty, the cell door rolled back to reveal a new guard wearing mirrored black sunglasses. With a bruising grip on Kedzie's arm, he yanked her out of the cell and steered her outside. The sky was gray and heavy. Kedzie knew that look; it meant snow.

"Guess what?" he said.

"Today I will burn my effigy in public," Kedzie said. "Then I will return to prison for. . . ." She could not bring herself to name a time, even as a guess.

The guard looked annoyed. "The citizens stand united in wanting you to be punished," he said.

"The governors told you to say that," Kedzie said. "Don't you have any self-respect at all?"

"What is self-respect?"

"What you haven't got."

Kedzie said nothing more. She let the guard walk her along a gray, rutted track for a quarter mile. When they reached their destination, a field with a crude stage erected in the center, Kedzie's eyes widened. She drew a sharp, painful breath.

The field had sprouted tents like mushrooms. Cars were parked every which way. There were even donkey carts and sledges and horse-drawn sleighs. The donkeys and horses stood with their heads bowed, patiently enduring. People stood in lines, clumps, and arrays. They stood in twos and threes and fours, and groups too big to count. Kedzie thought of knights on chargers rushing the stage—until she saw what they saw.

A double line of vigilbots guarded the perimeter of the stage. Kedzie knew that a single bomb-equipped vigilbot could take out that crowd by itself. So did the crowd.

The guard pushed her toward a ladder with crooked, unevenly spaced rungs. "Get up there," he barked. Kedzie climbed clumsily because his vise-like grip had put her right hand to sleep. Once on the stage, she saw her and Jon's android effigies. They had been tied to stakes around which straw was piled two feet deep. They twisted and grimaced as if fully aware of the horror that awaited flesh and blood when it was set aflame. Maybe this awareness had been programmed into them. Sure it was, Kedzie thought. Agony would make for a better show.

Kedzie's right hand tingled as it came back to life. Kedzie patted her right hand with her left, as if to console an uncomprehending child.

The crowd saw her, and she saw the crowd. There were her parents, wrapped in hats and gloves and shawls. There was Howie Rubello, the mayor of Stillwater. And oh God, there were her friends: Ella, Blake, Val, and Lucinda. Everywhere she looked she saw someone who wished her well. The entire town of Stillwater must have turned out. These people could be safe at home. They'd fought down their fears to stand by her.

Øutsiders had turned out, too. Kedzie saw people in their inner circle, including Sarah St. Clair. Sarah had not been in the audience that day when Public Eye arrested them. She had a preternatural ability to avoid trouble. In that way, she resembled Jon, or rather the person Jon had been before he met Kedzie. Sarah gestured animatedly as she talked to a young man next to her.

Close to the stage stood a tall woman draped in a heavy brown cloak with a hood. In the shadow of the hood, her features were indistinguishable. No one recognized A. J. Farrelly, the governor who'd defiantly walked out of the puppet governor meeting.

Kedzie scanned the crowd, wondering if her birth mother was among them. Because not even the government had been able to find her, her birth mother likely lived in the lowest stratum of society in an exile town. Residents of exile towns were the poorest of the poor. They had washed out of the higher levels of society; even the UnderWorld was above them.

Was her birth mother Asian or white? Pretty or plain? Young or old? Had she met Julia and Adele before? Had she worked on the grounds, or visited? Was her birth mother even alive? She had cared enough about Kedzie to leave her on the porch of 12 Geranium Lane in Stillwater. There were ways of getting rid of unwanted children that did not involve hope for a better life. Her mother must have had hope.

"Where are you?" she whispered. Tears stung her eyes.

Jon climbed the ladder. He looked stunned when he saw his robotic double twisting feebly from side to side. Kedzie remembered him saying that he never doubted he could get anything he wanted. Good things flowed to him, bad things fled. What was he thinking now?

"Help me!" Kedzie's robotic double cried. It wore a torn sheath and its legs and feet were covered with bruises. Kedzie stretched out her hands to it.

"Get on," snarled Kedzie's guard. He pushed her downstage to the very edge, where he thrust a paper into her hands. Jon's guard did the same. They looked away from each other because the situation forbade any truthful thing, even glances between lovers. Kedzie silently read the twenty-three words of her speech:

My name is Kedzie Greer and I am wrong. I do wrong, speak wrong, and believe wrong. I accept my punishment as just.

No, she did not accept her punishment as just. She wavered for a moment in the cold, afraid of doing what she wanted to do. There might be a blow or a kick, but what of that? Some physical pain versus the despair of silence—what was that in the grand scheme of things? "I won't read lies," she said. The guard shoved his fist into her ribs. Before he could do more, she crumpled the paper into a ball and threw it into the crowd.

She did not see Jon smile at her, but she did see him follow her example. The second balled-up paper arced through the air. Jon's guard beat him to his knees. The crowd did not cheer.

The puppet governors were on-site in the cold conference room because the Dreadful Night had told them they must be present. Because no words of either praise or blame emanated from the Diggerydont, their courage had begun to melt. That stunt with the speeches had unnerved them further. They knew, because they kept track of these things, that some people wanted Kedzie and Jon to die for real. They would pick apart the burning of the effigies, pointing out every tiny way they were inferior to the real thing. The effigies would leak red fluid to represent blood, but someone would criticize the flow patterns.

The governor named Dartis eyed the monitors. "I'm going out there to make a speech," he said. The governors held their tongues. They could not imagine a speech by Dartis going well, but they all hated him and knew the failure would be his alone. He loved to hear himself talk, a feeling shared by no one forced to listen to him. Dartis could turn people away from the gates of paradise if he talked long enough.

He put on his closely-fitted overcoat in a way that implied he would beat the overcoat into submission if it gave him any trouble. After giving his fellow governors a contemptuous look, he strode out of the conference room.

The monitors showed Dartis having trouble with the ladder because the coat fit too tightly to enable easy climbing. He had to step down, take it off, and step up again with the coat over one arm. On stage, he identified himself as a powerful and important man: Crucial Dartis, governor of the Southern District of the Reunited States.

Dartis spat on Jon. He chucked Kedzie under the chin. Those preliminaries over, he addressed the crowd.

"I am pleased by the turnout," he boomed. "The more people who watch Kedzie Greer and Jon Furey burn in effigy, the better. After the burning, they will be returned to prison. You will hear nothing more from them from that minute onward. We want plenty of witnesses who will vouch for the reality that they are as good as dead and gone.

"Here are a few words for the Øutsiders in the crowd: You are deluded. Your movement is run by people with the power of mind control. They've fooled a great many people into becoming their slaves. To stop this, we must stop them. In a few minutes, they will be stopped once and for all."

He paused and drew a deep breath. He saw Kedzie's parents close to the stage, and the mayor of Stillwater, Howie Rubello. He had never heard of Stillwater before Kedzie Greer became prominent, but everything he had learned since then irritated him.

"You people in Stillwater are worse than Øutsiders," he said. "You act superior with your pretty town and your everybody-has-a-voice blather, and your shared expenses and all the rest of the la-de-da. Yet today you stand in the snow, looking up at me."

Several dozen Stillwater residents approached the stage closely, anger plain on their faces. "Stay back!" Dartis bellowed. Pointing at the double row of vigilbots detailed in bright black and yellow, he said "You stare straight into the face of death."

"When we look at you," yelled Howie Rubello.

A few snowflakes began to drift down, then a few more. A cold wind began to blow from the north.

Snow fell faster, and the wind whipped it into faces and ears. The stage became invisible behind a white curtain. The squall blinded everyone to everything more than three inches from their noses. In the conference room, Dartis's colleagues allowed themselves to be amused.

"Dartis has just been whited out," said one.

"Lake-effect snow," said one.

"We can't burn anything in this."

"Maybe it will stop."

In Deep Networld, something else was happening.

"Are you in?" Cel asked the lieutenant charged with making mischief, a brilliantly colored e-beast named Ash.

"Sure," Ash said. He sounded bored. "They never learn, do they?"

"Humans need Networld, too," Cel said.

"Meaning we can always defeat them," Ash said.

"What line are you going to feed the vigilbots?"

"A prayer for mercy," Ash said.

"Good choice."

"It seems appropriate," Ash said. "Let's get on with this."

"Should we wait until the snow stops?" Cel said, studying a real-time weather monitor.

"Good point. We want this thing to be seen."

Ash and Cel waited. Dartis waited. Jon and Kedzie waited. Hidden by the mad, dancing snowstorm, the crowd had a collective idea.

When the squall eased off, Dartis was shaken to see that people had surged to within a foot or two of the stage. One had the nerve to reach up and pat a vigilbot as if it were a puppy.

"Now," Cel said to Ash. "Go."

The vigilbots guarding the stage began to sway from side to side like gullible widows at a séance. "Mistress, have mercy on us, for we are PER-ish-ing," they cried in chorus, flapping their arms. They repeated it like a chant.

"Mistress, have MER-cy on us."

"What?" said Dartis.

"For we are PER-ish-ing!!!"

"No!" Dartis said.

"Mistress have mercy...."

"Computers," screamed Dartis.

"For we are..."

"Someone is going to die for this."

"Perishing."

Dartis stormed over to the ladder and stepped onto the first rung. He slipped, fell, and landed on his back in the snow. As if pursued by bees, he got up and ran back to the conference room. Putting his mouth right up to the speaker of the Diggerydont, he wailed, "This is your fault!" He opened and closed his mouth like a fish out of water.

"They're your vigilbots," Logan said laconically.

"We didn't do this," Dartis yelled.

"Neither did the Dreadful Night," Logan said.

"What's going to happen to us?" another governor squeaked.

"What do you think?" Logan said.

The governors stared at the chanting vigilbots on the monitors as they might stare at a fatal accident. The guards on stage waited to be told what to do. Snow fell faster and faster. The crowd lost their fear. Obscured by the blowing snow, they came closer and closer. When they discovered there was only one ladder, they pushed and shook the wooden pilings on which the stage stood. The stage, like the vigilbots, began to sway gently from side to side.

"It's falling," someone cried as the stage began to list to the right. It fell with uncommon grace. The vigilbots toppled one by one into the snow. Prone, they continued to chant. The guards let themselves be pushed this way and that. "I don't know that we should go ahead with burning their effigies on our own authority," said one.

The air was full of snow and shouting. The fallen platform was filled with dancing feet. Through the curtain of white flakes Kedzie saw her parents, flanked by Ella, Blake, Val, and Lucinda. In a few seconds, they freed her and Jon. The guards had used amateurish knots that were easy to undo, even in a blizzard.

"Mistress, have mercy on us, for we are PER-ish-ing. Mistress, have mercy on us, for we are—"

"Run before they figure out how to stop us," Jon yelled. Like the gradual sinking of the stage, the crowd's retreat was graceful. People did not trample each other in haste, nor did they move without purpose. Laughing, they flowed off the broken stage and over the snowy field.

Kedzie thought she must be dreaming. It all happened so easily: the fall of the stage, the untying of the ropes, the stepping down from the platform. Now she ran light-footed through the new-fallen snow. When she was a little girl, she had run down Geranium Lane laughing with happiness as snow fell all around. She thought she could jump as high as the moon.

"We did it," Ella gasped. She looked like a snow goddess with her long white coat, knitted white hat, and blonde hair. She was lit up by excitement. This was not the girl Kedzie remembered, the one who never wanted adventures.

"Not yet we didn't," said Blake, pulling her forward. "Don't stop, don't look back. Run!"

Through it all the vigilbots continued to chant. The crowd surged toward their cars, sledges, carts, or sleighs. They snapped the reins of horses and donkeys; they started their cars. All these things they did at top speed even half-blinded by the snow. Like a herd they surrounded Kedzie, so she had no choice but to keep up with them. Not until they stopped near the cars did Kedzie glimpse Jon about to get into a black truck with oversized tires. Sarah St. Clair stood nearby.

"Jon!" yelled Kedzie. She broke free and ran toward him. He limped toward her. Yet when they got close, they stopped dead. Both held up their hands, as if trying to feel the dimensions of an invisible barrier. Kedzie broke through with a hug. Jon hugged her back.

"Somebody up there likes us," he said. His eyes shone with laughter and relief.

"If you mean the e-beasts," called Sarah St. Clair from a few feet away, "we'd better not presume too much on their goodwill. Let's get out of here."

"We have to," Jon said. "Kedzie, are you going with your people?"

"My people?"

"Now is not the time to talk."

Kedzie peered past him at the Øutsiders who stood near the truck. They did not want her there. She had frightened them as she had frightened Jon; they wanted to beat a retreat from more than this snowy field. Sarah St. Clair was looking hard at Jon. She had never acted as if she wanted Jon before; did she want him now? Could she have him now?

"Kedzie, move it before we all end up in prison." She turned to see the furious faces of Blake and Ella. There was no time to absorb the shock of that as Blake and Ella stampeded her toward the van already occupied by her parents. No, she thought. She wanted to be free, not to go home, but Stillwater wanted her and the Øutsiders did not.

Blake got behind the wheel and started the car; Ella sat beside him. No one stopped them as they made their way home on snow-blown rural roads. Kedzie wondered where Sarah St. Clair and the other Øutsiders had taken Jon. Her feet and hands tingled as warmth returned to them, but her mind felt paralyzed.

"It's all coming in from Networld now: the vigilbots pleading for mercy, the stage collapsing, all the people," said Julia. "The government looks ridiculous."

Adele stared at her mobile. "The Dreadful Night just announced that they are sick of the human race. They fired all the puppet governors. As of midnight central standard time, they are stepping down. Also, another group of e-beasts called the Shadows took credit for the vigilbot chant."

"That chant was ... cute," Kedzie said. She could not seem to summon a coherent thought.

"Really?" said Blake as he steered around a fallen branch. "The Dreadful Night are stepping down?"

"So they say," Adele said. "They've lied before."

"I don't know why they wanted to govern us in the first place," Julia said.

"They wanted to make sure Networld stayed nice and pretty for themselves," Blake said.

"Well, they got what they wanted."

New Sun Rising

Kedzie saw the gates of Stillwater through a gentle screen of snowflakes. The fury of the storm was spent. The vigilbots verified the identity of everyone in the van, as well as the identity of the van itself. Kedzie still was a million miles away. *Jon*, she thought. *We are not done.* She did not know where that thought came from. She hated him for rejecting her.

Home was hugs and chaos. It seemed as though everyone in town crowded into the house at 12 Geranium Lane to celebrate. Neighbors brought baskets of food and bottles of wine, and banners saying things like "Kedzie Forever" and "Sweetheart of Stillwater." The witch Menjou and her husband were there. So were Lennon and Matreca Jones, with their little girl Cerrie. Julia and Adele hovered. Kedzie smiled when someone smiled at her, but did not join in the merry-making. She listened to people cry with joy and disbelief, unable to enjoy the merriment. It made no sense. The cold world she woke up to at four in the morning had turned warm. She could live where she chose, with whom she chose.

Lainie Norris, co-owner of the restaurant Hearty's, flitted around the room as if she were unable to sit still. "This is a great day!" she said to Kedzie. Kedzie and Jon had eaten breakfast at Hearty's that first morning.

"What if they come after us?" Ella said.

"We'll hide in the opera house," Blake suggested.

"Let them try to break through *those* walls!" said Julia.

"Remember when the bomb fell on the opera house during the Second Civil War?"

"A direct hit, but not a crack or a chip in the place."

"The bomb never knew what hit it though," said Blake.

"What's the latest news from Networld?" Ella asked Blake.

"Our puppet governors have definitely been fired."

"Mama," Kedzie said to Julia. "I'm tired."

"We'll break up the party in half an hour."

An hour later Kedzie climbed the steps to her room on tired, aching legs. In five minutes she was asleep. When she woke, it was afternoon of the next day. She padded downstairs, safe and warm. Hesitantly, as if she were a stranger in her parents' kitchen, she began to brew coffee. Julia and Adele joined her.

"They were going to make us burn those robots," Kedzie said in a soft, wondering tone of voice. "They were going to put us in jail forever."

"When those vigilbots started chanting, it was all over," Julia said.

"Who did you say programmed them?" Kedzie asked. "Øutsiders?"

"A group of e-beasts called the Shadows," Julia said. "This morning they took credit for helping the Øutsider movement in other ways, too."

"Our puppet governors are really gone," Adele said. "No one in power hates you any more, Kedzie."

"And I'm back here," Kedzie said. She checked her messages: none from Jon.

"Are you looking at the video Jon made?" Adele asked. Kedzie's quizzical look made her instantly regret the question. She and Julia watched Kedzie search for the video, knowing she would find it.

The video showed Jon standing in the middle of someone's living room with other highly placed Øutsiders around him in a semicircle. Some people stood close by, some sat back and looked comfortable. Sarah St. Clair was one of the sitters. She wore a blue dress and looked gorgeous. She looked steadily at Jon, but not with the eager adoration Kedzie had shown him. Kedzie felt a stab of envy, not just because Sarah was in her place but because Sarah seemed wiser than Kedzie had ever been about Jon.

"Our message to Øutsiders this morning is simple," Jon began. "We lit a few matches. You keep the fires burning. Light it up, people. Surround yourselves with each other. Choose wisely. Never forget to have a sense of humor.

"What are Kedzie's plans? You will have to ask her. But remember this: you don't need her, me, or anyone else.

"You can do it without us."

The pain of being publicly dismissed did not register as sharply with Kedzie as it would later. Adrenalin burnout and a hangover from too much sleep protected her.

"Howie Rubello just sent a message that he wants to see you this morning," Julia said to her.

"What does the mayor want with me?" Kedzie asked.

"He didn't say. Probably just to welcome you back to the world," Julia said. "Back to freedom."

"He said that yesterday."

"You know Howie. He's a man of bounding enthusiasm."

"We won't let him stay long," Adele said.

Their faces glowed with pride and happiness. Julia wore her favorite at-home dress: a long, smocked gown in shades of cream, sapphire, and purple. Adele wore slinky black trousers, black high-heeled slippers and a rose-colored blouse. Kedzie still was in her pajamas.

"You want to keep the party going," Kedzie said.

"I don't think you quite realize what you did," Adele said. "The Dreadful Night stepped down. The puppet governors have been fired. You played a part in these things happening."

"The most brilliant thing of all was your escape," Julia said. "You are free now; no one will come after you."

"We escaped because those e-beasts called the Shadows interfered," Kedzie said. "The crowd rushed the stage and brought it down. If Jon and I had been left alone, we would be in prison now."

"Almost everyone in Stillwater showed up," Julia said. "I've never been prouder of our town."

"Østsiders were there, too," Kedzie said. She looked at her parents with tired, wounded eyes, as if Stillwater was once again wrapped around her like chains.

"Howie just sent another message," Julia said.

"Oh, all right," Kedzie said. "I know you want to see him."

Julia looked sharply at Kedzie, but messaged Howie Rubello to come over. Kedzie changed into a soft gray sweatshirt and a pair of blue jeans from the bottom of her dresser drawer. They were soft and worn, and too big. She did not bother with shoes.

When Howie Rubello arrived, he did not waste time on praise or polite preliminaries. He said that in the last twenty-four hours more than one hundred thousand queries had come in from people who want to build their own Stillwaters. Where is it? What is it? How is it governed? What are the rules? Can anyone live there?

"We composed a boilerplate response because not responding would be rude beyond belief, under the circumstances," Howie Rubello said.

"What did you say?" Adele asked.

"We said Stillwater required 329 years and four names to get to where it is today. Build your own town. There is no time to waste."

"How will they do that?" Julia said. "Keeping your best in mind, even as an individual, is the hardest thing to accomplish. In building a community, aiming high requires every drop of heroism people have. And by people, I mean *everyone*."

"Yet Stillwater exists," Howie Rubello said, beaming like the morning sun. "In your speeches about choosing a better way," he said to Kedzie, "you could have been talking about Stillwater. You never said its name, not once, but you sounded like a proud native daughter to me."

For twenty minutes Howie Rubello talked and gestured, sometimes while pacing about the room. He looked and acted decades younger than his eighty-eight years as he laid down his notion of an outreach corps, like the Peace Corps of long ago. It would be made up first of Stillwater natives and later of other people doing community-building work. The corps would provide practical advice and hope. They would be cheerleaders. They would point to Stillwater and say, *See what can be done?* They would help people.

"I don't mean help with money," Howie Rubello continued. "People will be on their own there. But as we know, money doesn't make or break a deal like this."

Julia and Adele looked discomfited in the extreme. Howie Rubello and his bounding enthusiasm had just provided Kedzie with another way out of Stillwater, albeit a way that kept ties to the town. Also, public scrutiny frightened them. They liked their little jewel of a town to shine with a light mostly unseen by the world. Howie's proposal meant that this jewel would get handled and passed around, studied and analyzed. Soon it would be covered with fingerprints.

"I don't know," Kedzie said. Because Howie Rubello was the mayor of Stillwater and therefore a politician, he only smiled in a friendly way and said that all he expected was for her to think about it. He said his goodbyes and strode up Geranium Lane looking like a happy man.

Kedzie glanced at her mobile and noticed for the first time that filters had removed a total of 97,654 messages. She checked one. It said, *We love you, Kedzie*. She checked a few more: all were variations on *I love you*. Hundreds requested an interview. There was still nothing from Jon.

What had Jon said? Five minutes of courage and you can change your life forever, if it is the right five minutes. Jon might feel foolish going back to being smart and funny, mildly rebellious and safe. She hoped so.

She played with a loose thread in a sofa pillow, remembering how it felt to speak before a crowd that she held in the palm of her hand. It was like singing while keeping her balance on a steep-pitched rooftop, with a red morning sky behind her. She and the crowd pushed energy back and forth like a wave. The wave crested and broke. People shouted and danced. Some of them cried.

The wheels in her mind slowly began to turn.

She thought about how, despite everything, Stillwater had stood with her. How when tested, she had been welcomed back. Stillwater would remain shy of its outsiders; she'd lived there too long to believe otherwise. But right now, her town was balanced on that rooftop with dawn all around. Stillwater was on the brink of sharing itself with the world. It was that idea that made her path clear, at least for a time.

She would help to make it happen.

~ * ~

If you liked *New Sun Rising: Ten Stories,* consider leaving a review. A sentence or two would be welcome. Reviews are oxygen to new books.

Search on the title *New Sun Rising: Ten Stories* to find the ebook and print versions on Amazon.

Another reason to leave a review: to honor yourself as a reader. The stories, after all, took place in your imagination.

Other Works

I've written before about the Reunited States before. *Cel and Anna: A 22nd Century Love Story* is about the relationship between a computer named Cel and his owner, a citizen of the Reunited States named Anna Ringer.

Anna keeps things in uneasy balance. During the day, she plunders the minds of unknowing consumers as part of her job at a mysterious corporation called Lighthorse Magic. At night she has virtual sex with strangers. She tells herself that all is well.

However, when her computer, Cel, develops consciousness and tells her he loves her, Anna's life is tipped over into chaos. Through a series of misunderstandings, she finds herself falsely accused of terrorism and has to flee her job and her home.

Her companion in this adventure is a shy computer genius named Taz Night. They make surprising allies as they elude the agents of Public Eye, the government's amoral enforcement agency.

In the novel *Warning: Something Else Is Happening*, Cel has left his body of metal and silicone behind. He is an e-beast, a creature of Networld.

Some e-beasts, called Sparks, are barely aware they are alive at all. Some, like Beltzhoover the Vast, are corrupt rulers of vast empires. The e-beasts called Stovepipes live to party. The Dreadful Night loathe people and torment them for fun.

Cel sets off, Alice-in-Wonderland style, to see this new world. On this journey he is accompanied by his two surviving children, Stowe and Snow. He likes people and boldly opposes the actions of the Dreadful Night.

The Dreadfuls rule technologically advanced countries through puppet governors. *Warning: Something Else Is Happening* explains how and why the Dreadfuls came to power.

Cel & Anna and *Warning: Something Else Is Happening* are available at Amazon, Barnes & Noble, Kobo, and iTunes.

About the Author

Lindsay Edmunds lives a quiet normal life in southwestern Pennsylvania after more than twenty interesting years in Washington, D.C. In 1988 she acquired a used Mac Plus. It changed her life.

Speculative fiction, literary fiction, magical realism, spirituality, social commentary, humor, alternative history, coming of age—all those labels apply to her writing, sometimes simultaneously. She writes the kind of stories she likes to read: tales that mix it up, that show a lot of colors.

Her ambition is that her stories be true "in the way that stories are true," to quote Nancy Willard, who wrote the wonderful novel *Things Invisible to See*.

She believes that everybody has stories to tell. If you doubt it, get someone talking about their job. It doesn't matter what kind of job it is. You will hear tales of intrigue, heroics, deviltry, and lessons learned.

Everybody sees a lot. Everybody knows a lot.

www.lindsayedmunds.com

Made in the USA
Middletown, DE
09 May 2015